D0975412

Violet Raines Almost Got Struck by Lightning

Violet Raines Almost Got Struck by Lightning

Danette Haworth

Walker & Company
New York

First published in the United States of America in 2008
by Walker Publishing Company, Inc.

Visit Walker & Company's Web site at www.walkeryoungreaders.com

For information about permission to reproduce selections
from this book, write to Permissions, Walker & Company,
175 Fifth Avenue, New York, New York 10010

Library of Congress Cataloging-in-Publication Data
Haworth, Danette.
Violet Raines almost got struck by lightning / Danette Haworth.
p.   cm.
Summary: In 1970s Florida, eleven-year-old Violet's world is upturned by the
arrival of a girl from Detroit who seems bent on stealing Violet's best friends.
ISBN-13: 978-0-8027-9791-9 · ISBN-10: 0-8027-9791-1
[1. Best friends—Fiction. 2. Friendship—Fiction. 3. Neighbors—Fiction.
4. Summer—Fiction. 5. Lightning—Fiction. 6. Florida—History—
20th century—Fiction.]   I. Title.
PZ7.H31365Vio 2008   [Fic]—dc22   2007049129

Book design by Daniel Roode
Typeset by Westchester Book Composition
Printed in the U.S.A. by Quebecor World Fairfield
2 4 6 8 10 9 7 5 3 1

I come from a long line of storytellers:
My dad was a big ham, and my mom remembers
things that never happened.
For my parents, Larry and Joan

And for
Brooke, Matthew, Zachary, and Steve
You know I love you

Violet Raines Almost Got Struck by Lightning

# 1

When Eddie B. dared me to walk the net bridge over the Elijah Hatchett River where we'd seen an alligator and another kid got bit by a coral snake, I wasn't scared—I just didn't feel like doing it right then. So that's how come I know just what he's saying when I see him in church, flapping his elbows like someone in here is chicken. When Momma's not looking, I make my evil face at him, but he just laughs and turns the right way in his pew.

I fold the bulletin and fan myself. Lord, it's hot in here. The windows are open but all that breezes in are a couple of lovebugs, landing in front of me on a lady's hair. I elbow my best friend, Lottie T., and point at the bugs. They crawl around and slip under a web of hair-sprayed strands. I start giggling and Lottie does too. Only we press the giggles down so instead of coming out of our mouths, the giggles shake our shoulders.

Taking a deep breath, I lean forward and then,

"AH-CHOO!" The lady's hair blows over in one piece like a typhoon hit it, and two black specks fly out. Lottie laughs out loud. When the lady turns around, I see she has devil eyebrows, the kind that go up in a point. I smile innocently. "'Scuse me, ma'am." She nods and turns around. I look at Lottie and laughter starts bubbling up from somewhere deep until Momma puts her hand on my arm, pulling me back in the seat. I look forward and try to pay attention.

The preacher's talking about how too much honey can make you sick, and I know it's true because I have put too much honey on my peanut butter sandwich before, and I just about puked. But I get that he's talking about too much sweetness is sickening. He doesn't have to worry about me. I am never too sweet to anybody.

Just then, the church doors swing open and slam against the walls. Everyone turns around. I squint, but all I can make out are two tall people and a girl; the sun blasting in from behind has turned them into figures of darkness.

"Welcome," the preacher says. He doesn't even sound annoyed. He smiles and steps down from the pulpit, standing on level ground with the rest of us.

The tall people step into the light and smile, their eyes darting around the sanctuary. The girl's hair is so blond, it's almost white.

"Well, come on up here and let everyone get a good look at you," Pastor says.

As they pass, I notice the man has on a full suit, right down to the polished shoes. The lady's dress flutters at the hem when she walks. She's wearing some kind of summer dress made of a gauzy material, and she has a white hat on top of her perfect hair. The girl is dressed just like her, but she doesn't smile or look around like the lady does. She walks like a sandhill crane, kind of floating, but with her nose up in the air.

Everyone in church watches them pass like this is a wedding or something. I can't really blame them; we don't always have strangers walking down the aisle, so it's kind of interesting. I just hope this don't make church run longer than usual.

Pastor greets them like they are long-lost friends. "Folks," he says, "I want to introduce our new neighbors, Brad and Meagan Gold, and their beautiful daughter, Melissa."

Everyone claps but me. I don't know these people or if they deserve a clap.

Momma elbows me. "Violet," she says. "We must make them feel welcome."

I sigh and clap as ordered. But my clap is soft; my hands barely touch. If the whole church was silent and it was just me clapping, you wouldn't hear anything, that's how quiet my clapping is.

Pastor starts saying a few words about how they just moved down from a big city up north when Lottie shoves a note into my hand. *Don't you think she's pretty? She looks like a model! I wonder how old she is! Let's try to meet her after church!*

I scrunch my lips together. Three exclamation points in Lottie's note. I don't think the new girl is *that* pretty.

She looks like a goose neck, I write and pass the note back. Lottie reads it, shoots me one of her looks, and slides the note into her Bible.

When church is over, everyone rushes outside. As we walk out of the shade, the sun burns the part in my hair. Dust puffs up from the dirt parking lot and sticks to my legs. My head prickles with heat. I scratch it, but it's still prickling. I scratch again and then I hear Eddie laughing behind me.

I whirl around and almost bump into him, he's that close behind me. "What are you doing?" I say. I have to look up because he's taller than me.

He laughs again. "What's the matter, Violet? Did you think a bug was on you?"

I fold my arms. "No, just a bug *behind* me, a big stinkbug!"

He laughs. I can't ever seem to cross him.

In the parking lot, Lottie and some other kids swarm around the new people like they're movie stars. Melissa's taken off her hat and turns the brim around and around with clenched fingers. I'm surprised the straw doesn't break. I trudge over for a closer inspection.

"Violet!" Lottie's cheeks are pushed up by her big smile. "Violet, this is Melissa!" Lottie looks at me expectantly. I don't like how she introduces me to Melissa like something good's about to happen now.

Melissa looks at me and smiles one of those stiff smiles. Well, I can't hardly blame her. All these people clamoring around her like she is someone important. Since I am the leader around here, I decide to make it easier on her and I smile big, as if I mean it.

"Hi, Melissa." Okay, let's get this over with so's me and Lottie can talk about what we're going to do today.

"Hi, Violet," Melissa says and nods like she's approving something. "That's a pretty name."

I wasn't expecting that. "Thank you," I say. I do like her good manners. Maybe Lottie and I can show her around sometime, like in a few days or so when we're not busy.

I stick out my arm and shake her hand like I've seen grown-ups do. My grip is firm and so is hers, but it seems like she tightens hers, crunching my knuckles till they hurt.

I take my hand back and look at her. If she did it on purpose, she's good at hiding it.

Eddie asks, "Where'd you move from?"

I'm glad he's talking 'cause it makes it easier for me to watch her. Her lips are pinker than they should be. Lipstick! She's twisting her hat again, but she looks at Eddie and smiles. Their eyes are level with each other.

"Detroit."

"Where they make cars," Eddie says. "Cool." Eddie's smart like that, knows a lot of stuff. He was class president last year on account of his smartness and everyone liking him. I helped him draw his campaign posters, which said *Vote Florida Panther: Vote Eddie Brandon.* The panther part was my idea 'cause he's a fast runner, and all your U.S. president posters have either a donkey or an elephant on them.

Melissa shifts her body away from us. "Well, there's a lot more than car factories in Detroit. I mean, there's roller skating rinks, bowling alleys, the Pontiac Silverdome, and Lake Erie's not too far. Even Canada's close."

"You've been to Canada?" Lottie asks. Her voice spirals up and her eyes widen.

Melissa shrugs. "It's not a big deal."

She has just shrugged off an entire country. Lottie seems impressed.

I can't stand it. So I say, "Yeah, we got stuff like that here, plus Disney World." I act like it's no big deal even though I have never been there.

Melissa turns to me. "You've been to Disney?"

"Next year I'm going," I lie. Momma can't afford the tickets, but I can't let this girl win.

"I've been there twice," she says. "It's okay. Cedar Point's better."

My face goes hot. "When have you been to Disney?" I ask; she's just moved to Florida. But my question gets lost as Lottie presses in and asks her about Cedar Point and life in Detroit.

Just then, a shrill whistle cuts through the air.

Eddie turns and I do too. "My dad," he says. "See ya later."

"Bye, Eddie," I call out as he jogs toward his dad. Lottie yells good-bye too.

When I turn back, Melissa looks at me real curious. "He's cute. Is he your boyfriend?"

I almost choke. "No!" Most strangers ask if we're brother and sister, pointing to our dark hair and blue eyes.

Melissa takes this in like she's writing notes in her head. Then Lottie asks more questions. I want to groan out loud. I can't believe I'm stuck here listening to Melissa talk about living in Detroit, what a great city it is, how busy it is, how big her school was, brag, brag, brag. Then she says, "What do you guys do around here anyway? This place is like, in the middle of nowhere."

My eyes narrow. Do not insult the place of my birth. Mitchell Hammock is a good town. I take in her blond hair and her fluttery dress, which is a twin to her momma's, and her nylons and her dainty little high-heeled sandals, and I say, "There's plenty to do if you're not a priss."

Lottie gasps and her hand flies up to her mouth.

I see Momma heading down the dirt road, so I make a nice smile and give it to Lottie. "See you later," I say. I'll see Lottie at the fish fry. My eyes return to slits and I fix them on Melissa. Poison darts shoot from them, and I see that I have hit my target when she recoils a little. I turn and catch up to Momma, a real smile on my face now.

 2

It don't take long for Momma and me to walk home. We don't have a car 'cause then Momma would have to work a second job just to pay for it. Everything we need's right here in the neighborhood, anyways. Momma works in the bakery at Parker's, which is even closer than church, and every three weeks, the bookmobile stops in front of Parker's, so you got your library right here too. I even walk to school. Not next year, though. Next year is junior high and we get bussed out. I heard some of those buses have air-conditioning. I sure hope so.

When we walk into our house, we go around immediately and open all the windows and turn on the box fans. The breeze feels good. I quick go to my room and throw off my sticky church clothes and put on my cutoff shorts and a tank top. I can't get to the fish fry fast enough. Lottie and I are in charge of the dipping and frying, and there is nothing better than catfish fried in corn-meal. Best part of every Sunday is sitting at the Townsends' noisy table, eating fish and drinking iced tea. I like to pretend they're my family and Lottie and I are twins, the kind that don't look alike but are still twins anyways.

I come out to the kitchen. "Momma, hurry up!" I want to say good-bye to her properly, but if she doesn't hurry, Lottie might cut the lemons before I get there. I hope Lottie waits for me. She knows how I like to stick a lemon wedge in my mouth and suck the juice. We have contests to see who can last the longest. No one's beat my record yet.

"Momma!" God Almighty, the fish are gonna be fried and eaten if she takes much longer.

I pace around the table, then look through the window at Lottie's house. Mr. Townsend's cutting table ain't out back yet, so they haven't got started. Good. I don't like to miss anything. I figure I got a couple minutes still, so I pick up the newspaper from the table. Big black headlines shout this is going to be the worst hurricane season ever. They say that every year. I pass all those headlines and find the comics.

In the corner is what I'm looking for: *Today's Word.* Today's word is *taradiddle.* It means "fib" or "lie." The first part is pretty; the second part is just plain foolish, like you can't even believe that's a real word, and that's just what a lie is—something pretty you can't even believe.

Taradiddle. I like it. I tear it out carefully and add it to my word collection, which is in a shoe box sitting in the china cabinet reserved especially for this purpose. I put *taradiddle* right on top of *magniloquent.* You might think *magniloquent* is good since it sounds like *magnificent,* but it means that you talk in a stuck-up or highfalutin manner. Like if I was to use these words in a sentence, I might say, "Melissa is quite magniloquent. And that is no taradiddle."

"You can barely close that box anymore!" Momma says as she rounds the corner. *Finally!* She's put on a yellow summer dress and her hair's loose down her back. She lays her arm around my shoulders. "Going to the fish fry?" she asks.

"Yep." I buzz around her, pushing the shoe box back, setting the newspaper down, grabbing my flip-flops.

She yawns and stretches her arms. "I'm a bit tired. I believe I might take a nap."

"You sang real good today." I say this because it's true. Momma has the voice of an angel. But I don't slow down none. I know Lottie's waiting on me.

Momma smiles as I slide into my flip-flops. "You have a good time now. Be good." She squeezes me in a hug.

I laugh and wriggle out of her arms. "I'm always good!" I say. I blow her a kiss and fly out the back door to my best friend's house.

3

Mr. Townsend's fish-cutting table is all set up by the back door. He's kind of how I imagine my dad might have been except my dad died before I was born. The ice chest sits nearby, but no one's outside. 'Course I can hear all the playing and shouting going on inside. I walk up the concrete blocks and swing open the screen door. Lottie's little sister, Tootsie, twirls around the kitchen, bellowing a song I'm sure she's making up. There is so much noise, no one notices me at first. But I notice. I notice Melissa Gold sitting at the table with Lottie.

"Violet!" Tootsie runs up to me and grabs my hand. "Lissa's here!"

Lottie turns around and steps over the bench. They don't have a regular kitchen table—a wooden picnic table is what they eat on. They're so lucky. It's like summer every time they sit down to eat. "Violet, you're here!" Lottie says this like maybe I wasn't coming or something.

My eyebrows pull together. "'Course I am." But what I want to know is why is Melissa here. I give her a quick glance. "Hey."

She looks up. "Hi."

I don't smile and neither does she. Can't blame her—I did call her a *priss*, but she deserved it for calling this place *nowhere*.

"Lissa's from Troit!" Tootsie yells.

Lottie taps Melissa's shoulder. "Tell her." But before Melissa can open her mouth, Lottie's telling the story herself. "Detroit is the *murder* capital of the United States!" She flashes her eyebrows at me.

Okay, that is interesting. I would be willing to listen to that. I sit on the end of the bench real casual, and Lottie sits in the middle. Tootsie takes off my flip-flops and puts them on her own feet. Leaning around Lottie, I say to Melissa, "You ever see anyone killed?"

"Not me," she says, then she looks at Lottie. "But a girl I knew, her uncle had a cousin who worked in a drugstore and someone got shot there."

I snort loudly.

She folds her arms. "It's true."

"Yeah, but it's not like you saw it happen or anything."

She stretches her neck, just like a goose. "Well,

I wouldn't want to." She shudders like she's seeing it right now. "If a murderer knew you saw him, he'd track you down. You'd have to go into one of those witness protection programs and change your name and move and everything."

I think on this. She's right. I wouldn't want to change my name or move or anything. I like things just the way they are. I want to ask about the girl with the uncle who knew the cousin in the drugstore, but Tootsie grabs my hand. "Come on, Violet. Play in my room."

"I can't right now," I say.

"Play dolls with me."

Melissa's eyebrows go up. My face flushes with heat. Normally, I don't mind playing dolls with Tootsie, but I don't want Melissa to think I'm a baby.

"Violet's talking with us," Lottie says, pulling Tootsie's hand out of mine. "Besides, she didn't come here to play with you, Tootsie-Tutu."

Tootsie lays her head in my lap. Her curls spill all over my legs. "Please."

Lord, she's like my own little sister; I can't hurt her feelings, but at the same time, I don't want to be upstairs playing dolls while Melissa's got Lottie all to herself. "Tootsie—"

Her voice comes out muffled. "Please."

I sigh and push her head up. I say to Lottie, "I'll be right back—don't start frying without me."

"I won't," Lottie says. She leans toward Tootsie. "Violet can only play for five minutes, okay? Then you have to let her come back down."

I swear Melissa looks relieved when I let Tootsie drag me out of the room. After we leave the kitchen, Lottie and Melissa start talking and then Lottie giggles. I lag behind Tootsie on the stairs.

❦ ❦ ❦

I'm sitting on Lottie's half of the room while Tootsie arranges her dolls in a circle. They're having a fish fry. Apparently, some of the dolls don't like each other and are arguing with Tootsie over where they should sit.

Running my fingers over Lottie's footboard, I feel for the words Lottie and I scratched into the wood when we were six. Lord Almighty, did we get in trouble for that. Even though Mr. Townsend did his best to cover them up, the words are as plain as the nose on your face: *I love you Violet. I love you Lottie.* We have known each other all of our lives; our parents were neighbors before we were even born. My fingers trace the letters. I hope I'm not missing out on anything downstairs.

Tootsie thrusts a doll at me. It's the one with purple eyebrows. "You're this one. You're from Troit."

"I don't want to be from Troit." I smooth Purple Eyebrows's hair. "I'm from here."

"No!" She slips her thumb in her mouth, just like Lottie used to do when we were little. Back then, I carried a baby blanket everywhere and Eddie had a fish doll. He twiddled the fins so much he wore them right down to threads.

Momma's got my blanket in a keepsake box along with cards and drawings I've made for her. And I bet Eddie's momma's got that fish doll, too, because even when you outgrow your childish things, someone saves them for you. Someone who loves you does that so you don't forget who you are.

I'm still holding Purple Eyebrows when Lottie hollers up for us to come down. It's a bull race, me and Tootsie in the lead and Lottie's middle sisters, Hannah and Ashley, thundering down behind us. The grown-ups come in, and the noise level goes up about a thousand decibels.

Mr. Townsend slaps me on the back. "How ya doing, Vi?" He grabs his knife sharpener off the counter. "Time to get this show on the road," he says and heads out the back door with Mr. Gold.

"Well, look at all these girls!" Mrs. Gold says. She looks at me, then turns to Mrs. Townsend. "Another one of yours?"

Lottie and her sisters are all dishwater blondes, but I like it that Mrs. Gold thinks we might be family.

Mrs. Townsend laughs. "Four's not enough? This is Violet, Lottie's best friend."

Hearing that, my heart bulges with gladness and it's all I can do not to look straight at Melissa. Instead, I step forward and shake Mrs. Gold's hand. "Momma and I live next door. If you're not late for church next week, you'll hear my momma sing."

Mrs. Gold chuckles. "Well, you're certainly not a shrinking violet, are you?" Mrs. Townsend laughs.

I don't know what she means, so I just say, "No, ma'am."

"Let's go see how Mark is coming along." Mrs. Townsend ducks out the back door with Mrs. Gold.

Hannah and Ashley start arguing about who has to set the table, and Tootsie marches around them with her hands on her hips and my flip-flops on her feet. I look at Melissa and Lottie sitting on the bench. Suddenly, I realize Melissa is staying for the fish fry.

"Violet, what's wrong?" Lottie asks.

I quickly rearrange my face into a friendly face. "Nothing," I say, even though my heart feels like it just got slammed. "Nothing at all."

4

Melissa's nose wrinkles as she looks at the tray of fish fillets Mr. Townsend has just cut and rinsed. She sits down on the bench while Lottie and I begin to press the fish into the cornmeal. I pick up a lemon wedge and drizzle the coating with juice.

"Lottie! You still got your watch on!" I point with the lemon toward Lottie's wrist. Lottie's watch has a diamond chip in it. You have to tilt the watch and catch the light just right so's you can see the diamond, but it's there. Her parents gave it to her for her twelfth birthday, on account of it being her last year before becoming a teenager. She always takes the watch off when we cook 'cause she don't want anything to tarnish it.

She washes her hands, unclasps the watch, and puts it aside. We drop the coated fish pieces into the kettle, careful not to plop them in because you're talking about a kettle full of boiling oil.

"Come on, Melissa, you want to help?" Lottie says. "It'll be fun."

Melissa shakes her head. Her mouth is turned down. "I can set the table—would that be okay?"

"The forks and knives are in that drawer," Hannah says, pointing. She grabs Ashley's hand and they run out of the kitchen.

I know why Melissa offers to set the table. What she really means is *I'm not touching that fish!* She's using manners to disguise it, but I'm on to her. I figure if she's going to eat it later, she can help cook it now. I pull her away from the silverware drawer.

"Come on, Melissa," I say encouragingly. "It'll be more fun if you do it too." I really do mean it—it would be fun to see her squirm. Lottie gives me an appreciative glance. She doesn't know what I'm up to, but we'll laugh about it later.

I take off my apron and hand it to Melissa. "So's you don't ruin your fancy clothes."

She has no choice. She takes my apron, stands, and puts it on. "Thank you," she says to me. Well, I've got to hand it to her, keeping her cool and her manners when I can clearly see how grossed out she is.

Lottie explains how to roll the fish and drop them in. Melissa picks up the first piece and her lips pull back as soon as she touches it. I laugh inside. By the look on her face, you'd think she was handling fresh roadkill. She holds the fish between her thumb and finger and lightly touches it to the cornmeal before slipping it into the kettle.

"Good!" Lottie says.

Melissa turns from the stove and says, "I don't think I can keep smelling this fish."

"Sure you can," I say. "Just breathe through your mouth." Before she can object, I say, "Now the second piece."

She turns back and picks up another piece, holding it away from herself like a dirty diaper. When she touches it to the cornmeal, I press her hand down.

"Eew!" Her hand flies up like it's been electrocuted, and she jumps back from the stove.

I almost laugh out loud.

"That was gross." She turns to me. "Why did you do that?"

Lottie is looking at me. She looks mad too.

I make a what-did-I-do face at her and turn to Melissa. "Haven't you ever cooked fish before?"

She hesitates, then goes, "Of course I have. Fishsticks."

I can't believe Lottie doesn't huff like I do on

hearing that. "Fishsticks? Fish don't come out looking like little bars." I cannot believe this girl. I grab her arm and pull her out the back door.

"Violet!" Lottie pulls fish out with the tongs, but she can't leave the stove with the kettle going.

Melissa wrenches her arm away as we get up to Mr. Townsend's station. Perfect. He's just made the first cut on a big one, right under the head. The fish's eye is wide and looking up. His mouth is gaping, like he was surprised to have been caught. Mr. Townsend turns the blade and pulls it down. He lifts the skin and meat as he cuts and the fish's belly is exposed. With his fingers, Mr. Townsend wiggles out the wormy-looking guts.

"Oh!" Melissa has her arm against her mouth.

She steps backward, but I pick up the dump bucket and show her. "See?" I shake the bucket. Guts and fish heads slide over each other. "This is what cooking *real* fish looks like."

She pushes away from me and runs toward the steps but doesn't make it. She vomits right there on the stairs.

"Melissa!" Mrs. Townsend runs to her. She sweeps Melissa's hair back and holds it while Melissa finishes up.

I put the bucket down and stare. I didn't mean

for her to puke. But if you think you're going to be part of a fish fry, you better know it ain't no fishsticks.

❧ ❧ ❧

Lottie's at the screen door watching the Golds leave. Mrs. Townsend hoses down the back steps as Hannah and Ashley run around. I'm pulling the fish out of the kettle; they've turned out perfectly. The Golds' motor turns on, and I hear the crunching of gravel as their car turns out of Lottie's driveway.

Tootsie clatters up the porch steps, throws open the screen door, and runs in. "They're gone," she announces. When no one says anything, she brushes by Lottie and grabs her hand. "Don't be sad."

Lottie pats Tootsie's head. "I'm not sad," she says. She lets go of Tootsie and tells her to tell their mom everything's about ready. Then she looks at me. "I'm a little mad." She walks up to where I'm laying the fillets on paper towels. She leans against the counter. "I know you didn't do it on purpose, but you were kind of mean to her."

My mouth drops open, mainly because I didn't think Lottie had noticed. But now I've got to defend myself. "Lottie," I say, peering directly into her eyes, "we were both showing her how to cook fish. You heard what she said—the smell was getting to her."

Lottie squints. She's not quite buying it.

"You're the one who wanted her to cook with us. I was just trying to be helpful—I even gave her my apron so her clothes wouldn't get dirty, remember?"

Lottie nods. "That *was* nice of you."

"So when she said that about the smell, I thought maybe she'd do better outside, that's all."

Lottie's face scrunches up. She needs one more push.

I shake my head. "I just feel sorry for her, living in the murder capital of the United States, going to school with such dangerous people."

Lottie's eyes go wide. "I know! I can't imagine living like that!" Her face is all lit up and I feel better 'cause she's not mad at me anymore. "She said they might even build a subway there!" She moves the fish to a serving platter and grabs the coleslaw from the fridge on her way to the table.

I bring the forks and knives. "Like in New York?"

"I don't know. She said the subway would be aboveground." Lottie shrugs. "Like a monorail, I guess."

Big deal, they have monorails at Disney. It's just a ride.

Tootsie and the rest of the family come pushing through the screen door. Everyone sits down, and after we say grace, we start passing around the food. I am surrounded by noise and family and it is as cozy as snuggling in your bed on a cold night.

5

I'm sitting on my porch in the morning when Eddie comes down the road on his bike.

"What're you doing?" he says, turning down our walk.

"I'm going to Lottie's later." But right now I know for a fact she's doing laundry—I saw the sheets out on the line. I hate folding clothes, so I sat with Momma till she went to work, then I came out here to sit. "But I'm not doing anything right now."

Eddie wipes his forehead with his arm. "Want to look for cups with me?"

If you return thirty BrainFreeze cups to the gas station, they give you a free BrainFreeze. I need a drink anyways. A root beer one sounds good. "Let's go."

Walking down the road is like walking inside an oven. The humidity presses the sun down on you, and the dirt road blasts the heat back up.

Eddie thinks our best luck for finding used cups will be where all the teenagers park, out by the county road. We go down a little ways and then turn left onto the fork that dead-ends at the woods.

The footpath is worn in good, lined mostly by palmettos and wax myrtles, a few scrub oaks. Definitely cooler under here. We walk single file. Sometimes Lottie comes with us, but usually she's stuck doing chores, what with her dad working at the repair shop and her momma getting stuff ready for the farmer's market. I like being outside with Eddie 'cause he knows scientific things about bugs and snakes, and he can catch a lizard as fast as I can. Besides, when Eddie and I are alone, I don't feel like we have to be talking all the time.

We duck under spiderwebs that stretch across the path over our heads. The woods are a busy place. Woodpeckers are drilling trees and squirrels are running along branches in the treetops. One ground squirrel picks up an acorn and darts up an oak; another squirrel chatters right behind him. They don't seem to take notice of us, and we keep walking. Finally, we spill out to the open area that runs along the river.

Eddie pulls a pack of pretzels from the pocket of his baggy shorts. He gestures with the bag. I shake my head. Shrugging, he crinkles it open. "How was the fish fry?"

My chest heaves with a big sigh. Just as I am about to tell the story, it spins around and turns into something different. This new version is better. I try it out on Eddie.

"Melissa puked something awful at Lottie's," I say. I remember Lottie's sympathetic expression toward Melissa and I try to imitate it. "Poor Melissa." I press my lips together and shake my head. We pass by turkey oaks and cypress trees. You can't see the river from here; the woods end on a ridge that drops down to the water. We go around the bend and the net bridge comes into sight.

"What was *she* doing there?"

I like how he emphasizes *she*—like even he knows that gooseneck girl didn't belong there. "Lottie's parents invited them over. We were showing her how to cook fish, that's all. We were trying to teach her everything. I even showed her how Mr. Townsend cleans a fish." I look at him straight on to see how he's buying it.

Eddie starts laughing.

I forget to keep the sympathy on my face. "What?"

"I passed Tootsie in the field." His eyes twinkle. I shrug one shoulder.

"She said you pushed Melissa's head into the dump bucket."

I stop walking. "What? I didn't do that. I didn't make her puke on purpose."

Eddie looks at me and grins.

"I didn't." I start walking again. The ground slopes up into a cliff along the river. The net bridge stretches between a dock on this side to a ramp on the other side. The boards you have to climb to get up to the bridge are a termite's dream, rotten and moist.

"Gonna cross with me, Violet?"

The bridge sags high above the river. Most of the netting has fallen off. The wires look thin. And there are gaps big enough for a person to fall through. Him and that bridge—he won't leave me alone about it.

"Let's take the long way around," I say. "Might see an eagle if we do."

Eddie stares at me, smiling. I stare back, daring him with my eyes to say something.

"Okay," he says. "Let me feed the fish first." He climbs up, grips the hand cables, and the wires shake all the way to the other side. The bridge squeaks and clanks with Eddie's first step. A thick cord runs on the bottom where there used to be boards to walk on. Eddie slides across it as easy as a tightrope walker.

I look around for a long stick. In case he falls in, I could hook his collar and drag him out before the alligators get him.

Eddie stops in the middle of the bridge and starts throwing pretzels. "Violet! Did you see that one?"

"No!" I can't see nothing through that black water. I do see bubbles and then pretzels disappearing suddenly, as if yanked down.

"Hey! There's Alfred!"

My heartbeat goes into a drumroll. I ain't moving any closer, but I stretch my neck and my eyes strain over the river. Those alligators are sneaky. They float with just their eye humps sticking out. Downriver's smooth as glass, and when I look back to Eddie, he's smiling and throwing pretzels. My heart calms down.

"Alfred?" I say, moving a little closer. "You mean Allie." We ain't seen that alligator since last year. Seen some baby ones, but not that big one. Lottie and Hannah thought it was a log, it was so far away, but Eddie and I know it was an alligator. We just can't agree on if it's a boy or a girl. 'Course I secretly think that gator's a boy, but I like to mess with Eddie about it.

"Oh, man!" he shouts. "You just missed the biggest catfish." He holds his hands about three feet apart.

I laugh. "You big liar."

"You ought to know," he says, coming off the bridge. It springs back after his weight and rattles before settling down. We start walking again.

I'm frowning now. "What do you mean?"

He leans his head toward me. "I know you don't like Melissa."

His words cut right through to my heart. Not because they are mean, but because they are true. I think how I might get around this, but Eddie's not easy to fool like Lottie is. He knows when I'm lying.

We walk in silence. The path is getting narrower again; we're getting close to the county road.

Eddie bends down and picks up a crushed BrainFreeze cup. "I wouldn't worry about it."

"I'm not worried."

He shrugs.

"I'm not—what would I have to be worried about?" I scowl at him.

He raises his hand like a stop sign. "Okay, nothing."

The way he says that gets under my skin, and I narrow my eyes. "What?"

"Well . . ." He pauses, scratches his neck. "Maybe you're a little jealous."

I cannot believe I'm hearing this. "Jealous! What would I have to be jealous of?"

He waves his hands around, erasing the air between us. "Nothing—forget it."

I stop walking and cross my arms. "Tell me."

Sighing, he turns around and faces me. "Well, she's pretty . . . Lottie likes her. . . ." He pauses. "And she wears a bra."

My face flashes with heat on that last word. My mouth drops open, but nothing comes out.

"But you shouldn't be jealous," Eddie says. How he can even talk after saying that one word is beyond me. "You got everything she does." He starts to walk, then turns around, and though his lips are straight, the tiniest bit of a smile shows through. "Except the bra."

I pick up a stick and hurl it at him. He raises his forearm and blocks it. I grab more sticks and become a human machine gun, *bam, bam, bam,* but he laughs and runs ahead.

"Come on, Violet," he yells over his shoulder. "We're almost there."

"I ain't going nowhere with you," I yell back. "I didn't even want a BrainFreeze!"

6

I'm so mad at Eddie that I cut through the woods, pass the bridge, and make it back to the road in just a few minutes. What does he know anyway?

I try not to think of it as I pound down the road, but that word keeps bubbling up in my brain: B-R-A. *Brassiere. Slingshot. Cup holder.* Nope, the thought of being hooked up in one of those harnesses does not appeal to me. I'm not jealous and now I'm even madder at Eddie for thinking I was.

As I get up by Lottie's yard, I see the sheets still on the line, waving in the breeze. Lord, that girl is moving slow today. I wish she'd hurry up. But I don't feel like doing laundry, so I keep marching down the road. I'll give her another half hour.

In the meantime, I'm getting hungry. I don't feel like eating alone, so I cut through some yards to Parker's to see if Momma can take a lunch break. The air-conditioning whooshes over me when I walk through the electric doors. Goose bumps pop out all over my arms. I head over to the bakery, and Momma sees me right away.

"Let me get the cookies out," she says, but first she leans around the corner and kisses the top of my head. She used to kiss my face, but I told her I was too old for that. She's allowed to kiss my head, but no other kissing. Don't even blow me a kiss; I'll just duck and the kiss will land on the wrong person.

She puts on those big oven mitts and pulls out trays of chocolate chip cookies. I have come at just the right time.

She disappears into the back for a moment and comes up front to me. "You come for lunch?" She's pulling off her apron, so I'm guessing she's hungry too.

I nod. "Maybe some egg salad," I say. "Maybe some of them cookies."

Momma laughs and we head for the deli.

❦ ❦ ❦

One egg salad sandwich, four dill pickles, and two chocolate chip cookies later, I'm walking much slower back to my house. I don't cut through yards on my way back, 'cause you got to be quick when you do that—people don't like to see you cutting through their property.

Purple and black clouds block out the sun. The air is heavy and still—it feels charged. Going to be some lightning soon. After looking at the sky, I give myself about fifteen minutes before the first strike. A turtle could make it to Lottie's in that time. Even so, I pick up my pace. I don't want to get rained on.

From down the street, I can see those sheets in Lottie's yard hanging on the line like big flags. I cannot believe she's not done yet. I shake my head. If I wait on her any longer, I'll be stuck home during the storm. Lord, I wish that girl would get it into gear. Now I'm going to have to help.

I knock and wait. She's got to be faster with her chores if she wants to do anything fun. We could have been playing tag or getting a BrainFreeze, or she could have had cookies with me and Momma. Oh, well. We can still have fun. Probably we'll play cards or games because that storm's coming and we'll be inside. I hope we play cards because I'm really fast at Spit and I almost always win.

I knock on the door again. If we play games, I got secret word tricks for winning Scrabble. Most people don't know that every letter of the alphabet is also a word, like the word for the letter *C* is *cee*. Put that word down, and they'll challenge you and lose their turn while you get points.

Mrs. Townsend comes to the screen door. "Hello, Violet!" She looks past me to the sheets. "I better get those in," she says and steps out.

"I'll get them," I say. Now I'm thinking if I do Lottie's work, she'll let me pick the first game. I step to the clothesline and help take down the sheets. "Is Lottie almost done?"

"Lottie's not home, Violet. She went to Sheldon's Discount with Melissa."

My mouth drops open. My hands freeze in midair. Sheldon's has your good stuff, like where you get your school clothes or a nice picture for your living room. "She went to Sheldon's? With Melissa?"

Mrs. Townsend still works the line, taking off clothespins and clipping them to her own shirt. "Mrs. Gold and Melissa came by a while ago and invited her. But come back later. She'll be home then."

My cheeks harden and the tips of my ears feel hot. A few sprinkles wet my face and then suddenly rain pours down. I bundle up the one sheet I've taken down and shove it into Mrs. Townsend's arms before running home.

I have misjudged the storm.

7

If Lottie thinks I'm going to show up on her doorstep, she is sorely mistaken. I won't call her, and she's afraid to call me. I know this 'cause the phone hasn't rung in two days. Serves her right. She wants to go off with Melissa, fine, but don't think I'm waiting around. I got lots of stuff to do.

Like right now, in the two days the phone hasn't rung, I have read three and a half books I got from the bookmobile. I cleaned my room—not shoving everything under my bed like how I usually do it, but actually sorting things out and putting them neat like how Momma likes it. I also pulled weeds from Momma's flower beds. I thought I'd let Lottie see me outside so she could come over and apologize, but that girl is ashamed enough that she couldn't find her way over.

I check the kitchen clock. It's almost three o'clock. My eyes are going to pop out if I read any more, and I'm wearing down a path to the window, where I keep spying on Lottie's house. I have decided that Lottie's sentence will be over at three. She has suffered long enough.

Lord, that minute hand creeps slower than a snail. I can barely take the slowness. Sweat trickles down by my ear. I've already shut off the fans and closed the windows so I don't waste any time getting over to Lottie's. Ten, nine, eight, seven—*c'mon, c'mon*—five, four, three, two, one. Finally! Three o'clock.

Gladness rushes over me as I dash out the door and over to Lottie's. I'll forgive her instantly. I'm not one of those to hold a grudge over someone who's truly sorry, and I know Lottie will be. We been best friends forever.

I raise my fist and knock on the door. We haven't driven Mr. Townsend's old truck around for a while. Today would be a good day for that. I knock again. Then I notice all the windows are sealed and the wood door is shut solid behind the screen. I pound on the door. "Lottie! Lottie!"

I don't hear even a whisper.

Backing off the porch steps, I look up to the bedroom windows. No sign of anyone. I back up a little more so I can see the whole house.

Nothing.

I have been shut out.

My heart hollows out, then hardens. I bet I know where they are. All laughing and having a good time with Melissa Gold. Lord, how I hate that girl. Marching back to my own porch, I kick up their gravel driveway, sending a spray of stones against their house. I didn't mean to hit it, but it's kind of satisfying because now I have hurt them, even if it's only their house.

8

I'm still sitting on the porch swing when a storm blows in. The sky is dark and moody—my feelings exactly. The air prickles. But it don't rain, not yet. The first lightning strikes the sky and I can barely say "one thousand one" before the thunder rumbles. You want to know how close lightning is, count "one thousand one, one thousand two," and so on after the strike until you hear thunder. Every "thousand" you count is a mile. This lightning's only a mile away. I rush inside and turn off the oven, which is heating up tonight's casserole. Don't ever leave your electric stuff on when lightning's close—it will blow up your house.

I shuffle back out to the front porch and sit down. The sky flashes and booms. Momma used to tell me thunder was just the angels bowling in heaven. You could always tell when the unskilled angels took their turns 'cause some thunder's quiet, and some's loud, like that particular angel got herself a strike. 'Course I know it's just a story to make little kids brave during storms. I just like to think of it sometimes.

Suddenly, rain bursts down and pummels the trees and the house. No warning to it, just starts full force like that. It's thundering and lightning, but I am safe and sound on my porch.

I'm sitting there watching the show when Eddie comes through the rain on his bike. Jumping to my feet, I yell, "What're you doing out there? Get up here!"

He dumps his bike and plods up the porch steps like a swamp monster. His sneakers make wet squishy sounds. He is soaked to the bone.

"Oh, my Lord," I say. "What are you doing in the rain? I know your momma taught you better than that."

"Oh, man," he says and shakes his hair. Water flies everywhere.

I flinch backward. "Quit doing that! I'll get you a towel. Don't you dare sit down till I come back."

After he scrubs himself dry, we sit on the swing. His legs are longer than mine, so he pushes the swing while I sit curled up on my side. The rain drums on the roof. Lightning sparks in the sky like fireworks.

"I give that one a seven," Eddie says.

I nod. It wasn't especially bright or loud. "Maybe just a six."

We watch, throwing out our scores after each strike.

"Eight," he says.

He's being too easy. "Seven," I say.

Then the air whooshes up like there's a big vacuum in the sky. I glance at Eddie, whose eyes look as big as mine feel, then static rushes over me, prickling my hair, and my heart jumps, but before I can open my mouth, a single bolt strikes and flares over the woods across the street and at the same time *BOOM!* like an earthquake.

My blood pumps like a fast-moving river. My heart races. I can't hear nothing and when I close my eyes, I see the bolt of lightning etched on the back of my eyelids. Eddie turns to me, his eyes blazing.

"I think that hit something," he says.

I nod. My hands are shaking. "Did you feel it?"

His eyes burn bright blue. "Yeah, I felt it."

"Me too." We look at each other in amazement.

The air around us is charged with electricity. I wait. Something big is going to happen, I just know it.

 **9**

After Momma leaves for work in the morning, I put on my best T-shirt and shorts and head outside. But don't even think I'm going to Lottie's. Oh, no—two can play at this game.

I'm going to Melissa's.

I walk real jaunty as I pass Lottie's. That way, if she looks out, she'll wonder why I'm smiling so big and why whatever's making me so happy has nothing to do with her. I keep it up until I can't see her house anymore.

Mrs. Gold opens the door after I ring the bell. She smiles. "I remember you; you're Violet, right?"

"Yes, ma'am." I smile back, putting on my fancy manners. "I came to visit Melissa." I lean and look into the house behind her. "She home? I mean, is she home?"

Mrs. Gold chuckles like I said something funny. She swings the door wide open. "Why don't you come in? Melissa will be happy to see you."

Yeah, I bet. But what I really say is, "Thank you." Goose bumps race down my arms, it's so cold in their house. God Almighty, most folks 'round here get by with open windows and fans, a window air conditioner for your bedroom if you really got to have it. But not the Gold family. I heard a lady in church saying Mr. Gold had central air-conditioning installed before they even left Detroit. It works real well, too—dries the sweat on my neck right up.

I expect Mrs. Gold to holler up the stairs like any normal person, but no—she walks all the way up and knocks on a door I can't see from where I stand. Their voices are quiet, except for the part where Melissa says, *"What?"* I kind of laugh to myself over that.

Mrs. Gold comes all the way back down and stands beside me. Melissa stops halfway down the stairs.

"What are you doing, honey?" Mrs. Gold asks. "You have a visitor. Come on down."

Melissa heaves her chest like this is the worst thing in the history of the universe anyone has ever had to do. I want to give her my evil face, but Mrs. Gold is standing right there. Melissa crosses her arms and trudges down the stairs.

"Well, you girls don't need me hanging around," Mrs. Gold says. "I'll be in the kitchen."

After she leaves, Melissa looks down at me. "What do you want?"

"How tall are you?" I ask.

She slits her eyes. "Why?"

I shrug my shoulders. "Just asking. But it don't matter, if that's private information."

"It's not private," she says, almost spitting on me. "It's just—never mind."

That's okay. I don't share information with the enemy either. I glance around the living room. It looks like a picture out of a magazine. Very pretty, I can admit that. "I like your house," I say.

"Thanks." Her arms are still crossed.

I am trying to like this girl—just a little bit—so me and Lottie can go back to normal, but I swear, she is doing nothing to help.

Mrs. Gold comes back. "What are you girls doing standing by the front door? Melissa, take Violet upstairs and show her your room. You girls talk and get to know each other. Go on!"

Melissa turns without saying anything and drags herself up the stairs with me following behind. We pass through some beads and we're in her room. It looks like a princess's royal chamber.

Everything's pink and purple and soft looking, like a dream.

"You got a TV in your room?" I can't believe it.

She cracks a little smile. "Don't you?" She sits on her bed and rattles off all her favorite channels.

I sit on the bed too, but on the end, so's I'm not too close to her. I keep my posture straight. "We got one in the living room." I shrug my shoulders. "But we don't get all those channels."

Her eyes practically pop out of her skull. "You don't?"

I shake my head and look at her bookcase, which has lots of decorations on it but only a few books.

"Why not?" Then her face changes. "Can't you afford it?" She says this softly, like someone has died.

" 'Course we can afford it." Which I don't even know if we can or not. "I prefer to read."

"Oh, my gosh! That's so . . . old-fashioned!"

I stiffen.

"I mean, no offense or anything." She reaches onto her nightstand and grabs a couple of magazines. "But TV is great." She opens a magazine and shows me a picture of some older boy. "Isn't he cute?"

I stare at the picture. "Yeah, I guess so."

She takes the picture back and hugs it to her chest. "My friends in Detroit and I *love* him! He's on *Paris Heights;* you ever heard of that show? It's a soap opera. I watch it every day with my mom."

When I shake my head, she says, "You really are living in the sticks. No offense."

I look at her bookcase again. "Well, *no offense,* but it doesn't look like you read much."

She jumps off the bed, grabs a stack of movie-star magazines, and plops them on the bed. "I read all the time."

"These don't count—they're not even real books."

"Oh, yeah?" she says and juts out her chin. "For your information, I'm going to be a celebrity, and I have already made lots of connections with important stars."

I don't know what she's talking about and I say so.

Opening a dresser drawer, she pulls out a stack of papers and plastic sheets with pages in them. She cradles them close to her chest. "What I'm about to show you are the results of my work."

I must look confused, because she explains, "I've written letters to important people in Hollywood to let them know I'll be available when I'm eighteen." She smiles all dreamy and sits on the bed. "I get so many letters back." She looks straight at me. "Not everyone gets responses, but my secret is I include a photo of myself—that way, they can see my potential. Here's one of my best."

I'm expecting a gooey bunch of *I love you* and *I'm your biggest fan*, but her letter mentions an episode of a show she watched and talks about it point by point. I don't know what the letter's about, but it sounds intelligent. I hate to admit it, but she writes pretty well. I hand it back to her. "Good letter."

"Did you even read it?"

"I perlustrated it." One of my newspaper words; it's a fancy way of saying I read it carefully. I like to sound intelligent too.

She gives me a strange look, then she goes on talking about her letter writing and that she sometimes sprays the envelopes with perfume, but how by far the best thing to do is to include a photo.

Her talk is boring. I interrupt. "So what's in those plastic things?"

"Photos from Hollywood." She hands me a big photograph and I see it's the same guy from the magazine. "Don't put your thumbs on it," she says. "Hold it by the edges."

I sigh but do it anyway. There's an autograph in the corner: *Love and peace!* and he signed his name. When I run my finger over it, I don't feel any grooves. "Did he really sign this?"

She frowns. "Of course he did. He sent it right after I sent him my letter."

"But you can't feel where he pressed the pen."

She snatches the photo back. "Okay, then look at these."

I read the first one, then a few more. They all kind of sound the same: *"Hey! Thanks for writing me!" "I'm glad you like the show!" "Fans like you make it all worth it!"* They try to sound friendly and cool. "But I don't see anyone offering you a script or anything."

"I should have known better than to think you'd understand." She stands up from her bed and carefully puts the Hollywood stuff back. "You don't even watch TV."

I stand up too. "So what? You don't even read books."

"You're weird."

"I know you are, but what am I?"

She rolls her eyes. "Still using baby stuff, huh? Lottie told me you were only eleven. I can't believe you're going into seventh grade."

That's 'cause I have a summer birthday. But since she called me a baby, I hit her with an oldie but goodie: "Want to lose ten pounds of ugly fat?" I ask. "Cut off your head!" I stay just long enough to see her face go into shock, then I turn and run down the stairs.

She races after me. Her mom must have heard us 'cause she comes out from the kitchen just as I put my hand on the front doorknob.

"Leaving already, Violet?" Mrs. Gold asks. She gestures with a plastic container of chocolate chip cookies. I recognize the Parker's label. "I was just about to see if you girls would like a snack."

"No, thank you, ma'am," I say and twist the knob. Melissa tries for a hard glint when I look up at her. It's pathetic. My left side makes my evil face at her; my right side is still polite to Mrs. Gold. "But I know those cookies are good," I say and open the door. "Because my momma made them."

Mrs. Gold's smile drops. I run out the door and all the way home.

10

Each day has its own troubles—I heard Pastor say that before. What he means is, don't mess up today by worrying about yesterday or what might happen tomorrow. So even though I'm still a little mad at Lottie for going with Melissa, I decide to start this day like nothing's happened.

So if nothing's happened, I'd go over to Lottie's, and that's just what I do.

"Violet!" She grabs my hand and pulls me into the house. "Where've you been? I've got so much to tell you!"

She's so happy to see me, that tiny bit of grudge falls off my heart like a clod of dirt.

We head straight to the bench under Lottie's stairs. It's our secret talking place. It's more like a cave, really, deep enough for an old storage bench and a rug. If you hide under the bench, no one thinks to look for you during hide-and-go-seek.

Lottie says she's getting too old for those games, but still, it's a good hiding spot.

Lottie's bursting to tell me something, I can tell. I can't help but lean in. "What?" I say with a smile.

Lottie widens her eyes. "I went with Melissa to Sheldon's the other day. She is so cool. We got hot pretzels, ate in a restaurant, tried clothes on, and—"

I develop a sudden coughing fit. "Water," I choke out. As Lottie fetches my water, I fume. I do not like listening to my best friend telling me what a good time she had with someone else.

"Where was I?" she asks after she hands me the glass.

"I don't remember." I take a long sip from the water. "But *I* got something to tell *you*."

"What is it?" she asks.

"Oh, nothing," I say, as if it's just the least little important thing. I pick some lint off her shirt. "Just me and Melissa are pretty good friends now."

She grabs my arm. "You are? What do you mean?"

I've got her now. Leaning back, I fold my arms behind my head and say, "We practically spent the whole day together yesterday."

A smile breaks over her face. "You did? Oh, my gosh! I was worried you wouldn't be friends. Now we could hang out together; we could be like the Three Musketeers." She claps her hands. "Tell me what you did! Isn't her room pretty?"

My face pinches together. I sit forward. This is *not* the reaction I expected. And besides, "When were you in her room?"

Lottie seems confused and leans away from me. "The other day. Mrs. Gold invited Mom and all of us over."

My eyes narrow a little and I nod. So I was right the other day. "Well, we had a great time." I say this because Lottie's not even acting jealous. "We talked about books and magazines and stuff, and she showed me all those letters she wrote."

"What letters?"

God Almighty, Melissa acted like she had the Secrets of the Universe in those plastic-encased letters. I can't believe she didn't force them on Lottie. Even so, I act like Lottie has totally missed out. "She didn't show you?"

Lottie shakes her head. "I barely had time to talk with her because of my annoying sisters."

I can't believe this! "They were in her room too?"

"They were maniacs," she says, rolling her eyes. "Touching everything, jumping on the bed.

Melissa only let them in because they promised they'd be careful with everything. It was so embarrassing."

I scrunch my eyebrows together. "So they were jumping. Big deal."

Lottie looks at me like I'm thickheaded. She fondles her watch. "You saw her room. It's not a little kids' play area—it's like a teenager room, for doing teenager things like painting your nails and writing in a diary."

"Oh, my Lord. That girl acts like the princess and the pea. Get one thing out of place in her room and *look out*! They're coming to arrest you."

Lottie shifts on the bench and folds her hands in her lap. "Well, I, for one, think it would be nice to have a room like that. And a little privacy."

What am I hearing? "Privacy from what?"

"Come on, Violet! I'm sharing a room with a three-year-old."

"So? You never complained before. Melissa's putting this idea in your head."

She shakes her head. "No, she's not. It's my own idea." Sighing heavily, she leans her head against the wall. "Sometimes I just wish I had a place to think. I wish I could leave my stuff out and not have to worry about it." She gestures at where we're sitting. "We have to sit here just to talk privately."

I like sitting on the secret bench. When I don't say anything, she goes, "You have your own room; you don't know what it's like."

Maybe I don't know what it's like, but I wish I did. I jut out my chin. "There ain't nothing wrong with your room. You're lucky to even have sisters. Melissa should shut her big, fat mouth."

"Don't say that. She's our friend now."

My lips open. My eyes blink. Then I say, "But I'm your *best* friend." And we're practically sisters. Suddenly I don't care to argue about Melissa or fancy letters or private rooms. I stand up and reach for Lottie. "Come on, I'll help you."

She looks frustrated and confused. "Help me with what?"

"Ain't you got some kind of chore to do?"

She sighs and grins.

That's how well I know her. A house full of chores is waiting on her and we'll take care of them together. She stands up and we head to the kitchen.

11

I'm conducting a dragonfly experiment on my porch: how close can I get to the dragonfly before he flies away? I'm already beating my own personal record, which is about three doormats away. I'd say I'm about two and a half doormats right now, and he hasn't even flicked a wing. The secret is to move slow, like you're not moving at all. It's taken me about fifteen minutes to get this close.

"Violet! Violet!" Eddie. I'd know his voice anywhere.

I slide my eyes up without moving my head. If I yell back, the dragonfly will take off and my experiment will be ruined. I continue to be a slow-moving statue. Eddie throws his bike down and pounds up the stairs. The dragonfly disappears.

I put my hands on my hips. "Do you know what you just did?"

He doesn't even pay attention to how he's ruined

my morning's work. "You know that lightning the other day?" He's talking loud and fast. His eyes are bright, like there's a light behind them.

"Yeah, yeah," I say.

"It hit the woodpecker tree!"

The woodpecker tree! No wonder there was such a loud boom. The woodpecker tree is a big, old tree in the woods across the street. You can hear them birds pecking at it every day. Even though the top of it got broke off in a hurricane, it's still one of the tallest trees in the woods.

My eyes get big and round. "Did it burn all the way to the ground?"

"No, but it blew the bark off!" He starts down the stairs. "Come on!"

We leave his bike there 'cause there ain't no way our bikes can make it through the woods with all those vines and roots. I can't wait to see a naked tree. "Let's get Lottie," I say.

So we swing by, Eddie repeats the story, and Lottie gets her momma to let her go with us.

Just a little ways into the woods and there it is, the woodpecker tree. I'm kind of disappointed. I thought I'd get to see what a tree looks like under all that bark. Instead, there's this strip about five inches wide from near the top of the tree all the way down, like someone took a huge potato peeler to it and peeled off one long strip.

"Wow," Lottie says.

I step up to it. Closer, I can see two gouges running inside the bare wood.

"Look at this!" Eddie picks up chunks of bark. "It's all over the place!"

He's right, bark and pieces of wood lay around in front of the tree like it exploded. One huge piece sticks out of the ground like an ax. Some of the bark is charred.

I put my hands on the tree and feel the wound. Closing my eyes, I can see that lightning strike again. This is one brave tree. It's still standing and most of its leaves are still green. The storm didn't knock it down. I'm glad now the tree isn't naked. Even this scar don't ruin its beauty. In fact, I think it gives it character, something most of your regular trees don't have.

We look around for a few minutes, then Eddie says, "Let's go to the cave."

"Sounds good to me," I say.

Lottie leans around the tree and peeks at me. "Would it be okay if we invited Melissa?"

I scowl. "She's not on the way."

"She's only a few houses down from the turn." Lottie says this hopefully.

She can tell I don't want old gooseneck. If I say no, she won't argue, but I don't want to seem like the kind of person who says no. "It's up to Eddie," I say. I'm counting on him being too interested in the cave to go even a little out of our way to pick up old Melissa.

But he shrugs and says, "Yeah, okay."

I jut out my chin and start walking. I hope she ain't home.

12

When Melissa opens her door, her eyes run over the three of us and she seems a little shocked. Lottie tells her about going to the cave and does she want to see it. Melissa's eyes land on me for a second. I try to look innocent while at the same time sending her a telepathic message: *Don't come. You do not want to come.* But my innocent face must be stronger than my telepathic powers because she smiles at Lottie and says, "Let me go tell my mom."

While Melissa's in the house, Lottie touches my arm. "Thanks for letting me invite her."

I didn't want Melissa tagging along, but even so, Lottie's gratitude annoys me. I lift one shoulder. "No big deal."

"Bet she's never been in a tree cave before," Eddie says.

Melissa pops out of the house. She's put on a

prettier shirt and brushed her hair. She's wearing little sandals with heels. "I'm ready!"

I don't think so. I point to her feet. "You can't walk in those. We're going up by the river."

"Isn't it paved?" She tilts her head. "They might pave by the river in Detroit."

"Well, this ain't Detroit," I say. "This is Mitchell Hammock. You better get your sneakers on."

"Might be a good idea," Lottie says.

Melissa looks down at her feet and then at Eddie. She smiles a little, like she's embarrassed. "Maybe I'll just wear these for now."

❦ ❦ ❦

"How much farther is this place?" Melissa is right behind Eddie on the footpath, Lottie behind her, and me last. That's how I like it— everything in front of me so's I can see what's going on. She brushes her arm. "I feel like bugs are all over me."

The real Melissa was a little fairy who lived in a forest; I learned that when we studied Greek mythology in school last year. Well, this Melissa don't know anything about being in the woods. Her parents must have forgot that part of their studies. But then I remember the Greek Melissa got turned into a worm and then a queen bee, so I guess her parents got it right after all.

"You shouldn't be scared of bugs," I say. *Since you are one!*

"Oh, please," she says without turning around. "You probably still catch lightning bugs."

As a matter of fact, I do. "Scorpion!" I shout.

"Aaah!" Melissa screams and stumbles backward into Lottie.

I walk up and pick up a twig. "Oops, my mistake." I toss the twig to the side and stand behind Eddie so's they can't see my smiling face.

Lottie chuckles. Well, I'm glad to see she ain't lost her sense of humor. I have to hang on to Eddie's shoulders, that's how hard it is to hold in my laughter.

"Violet," he says, quiet and low like he's correcting me. But I see his cheeks working into a smile.

Melissa glances at me and Eddie and a shadow crosses her face so quick I almost miss it. I've seen that expression on her face before, like she's filing information.

We start walking again. "Don't worry," Lottie tells Melissa. "There's nothing in here to hurt you."

"Coral snakes," I say. "Brown violin spiders."

"Alligators," Eddie adds.

This is too much for Melissa. She stamps her feet into position and halts. "That isn't true." She looks at Lottie. "Right?"

Lottie raises her eyebrows and shrugs like she's apologizing for the woods.

Melissa's eyes dart around the trees and then she fixes them on me. "I think you're right, Lottie. Nothing in here can hurt me." She tosses her head and starts walking again.

The hard ground we been walking on becomes muck as we get closer to the cave. I see Melissa's heels sink, but she don't complain. I have to give her credit on that, much as I hate to.

We're walking level with the river now. Cypress knees stick up out of the ground, some about two feet tall. I remember reading that gnomes were legendary creatures, probably based on cypress knees. I can see how that happened—the knees are all gnarly and misshapen, and they stand in groups. Like right now, they're all facing the river, silent, like they're waiting for us to leave so's they can continue their magical lives.

We get up to the cave, which is really a huge, old cypress tree that's hollowed out with a split big enough to squeeze into. The roots reach down around you and the top closes up over your head. Once, we got six kids in there.

Melissa scrunches up her face. "This is it?" She looks around at us. "I thought you meant a real cave. This is just a tree."

"You ever been inside a tree before?" I ask.

"I'm not going in there," she says. "It's probably filled with bugs and spiders."

I snort. "You're scared!" I step closer to the tree. "Well, I'm not." Just as I'm about to push forward, Melissa squeezes past me and into the tree. I stick my face up to the opening to see how she likes it. She pulls her shoulders in and her arms are clamped to her sides.

She shudders. "Move, move! I have to get out!"

I move aside and she ducks and squeezes out, shuddering all the way down to her feet. She laughs at herself. "I felt like a snake was going to drop on me!" She ain't even embarrassed, just being truthful. "It's dirty in there."

"It *is* kind of dirty," Lottie says, squeezing in. "But kind of cool, too."

There's plenty of room for me, so I slip through sideways. It really is like being inside a cave. It's so dark, I can't hardly see anything, but once me and Eddie came with flashlights and we saw that the top part is charred. Maybe someone lived in this tree and had campfires. Gaps at the bottom let a little light in and you can see through to the river. Sometimes, when the wind blows, it makes a sound like you hear when you put a seashell up to your ear.

Flecks of bark hang in Lottie's hair when we step out.

"I wonder if any criminals used this as a hide-away," I say as I pick the bark out of Lottie's hair.

"Where would they sleep?" Melissa asks.

Good point. Even I wouldn't lie down in that mud. Still, it could be a hiding place for gold or treasure. It could be a secret thinking place.

"Should we go now?" Melissa's already heading back the way we came.

"Want to see the bridge?" Lottie asks.

Melissa shakes her head. "I'm kind of itchy."

Lottie looks at me. "Should we go now?"

I shrug and step back into the cave. I'm not ready to leave it yet. I like the way the breeze sounds in here and how I can see the river through the bottom.

Eddie steps in beside me. I can barely make out his face. Our shoulders brush as he jostles in.

I bend down and point through one of the gaps. "Doesn't it seem like you can see clearer from here?"

Eddie crouches beside me. "Makes it seem secret."

Melissa bends in the doorway. She smirks. Raising one eyebrow, she says, "What are you two *doing* in here?"

We're standing alone in a tree. Heat flushes my face. I squeeze out of the tree, leaving Eddie by himself. My lips curl into a snarl when I look at her. "Nothing."

Melissa makes her voice smooth as syrup. "Are you sure?"

"Shut up," Eddie says, brushing himself off as he comes out of the cave.

Melissa turns. "Whatever," she says, walking past us to Lottie. Melissa hums quiet, but the kind of quiet humming that's meant for other people to hear. I recognize the tune instantly: *"K-I-S-S-I-N-G; first comes love, then comes marriage . . ."*

Heat deepens in my face. I cross my arms and press my lips together. I stomp down the path and don't even stop when Lottie shouts, "Violet, wait!" I especially don't stop when Eddie yells it.

13

I'm sitting in my pew, third row on the right, same as always. I don't see Eddie, and Lottie's not here yet, but Momma and I are always early on account of her being part of the choir. Before we left the house, I looked at *Today's Word*; it was *vicissitude*. This word has too many *S*s and sounds like a snake hissing. It means change. I didn't like it. I threw *vicissitude* out.

"Violet!" Tootsie runs down the aisle and climbs onto my lap. The choir members and musicians are warming up, so the sanctuary is filled with lots of different tunes. Service is fixing to start.

Lottie files into the pew, followed by the rest of her family. "Hey, Violet."

"New shirt?" My eyes run over the sequins. "I like it," I say. "It's sparkly."

"Isn't it pretty? Do you really like it?" She's about to say something else, but the choir bursts into song and we jump to our feet.

When the singing is over, Lottie gets real fidgety, looking around and glancing at her watch. The pastor is talking about how when Jesus chose his disciples, he gave some of them new names, like Peter, whose name used to be Simon. He gave them new names because they were now new people. I've heard this part before, so for the third time, I crane my neck to see what Lottie's craning her neck for.

I pass Lottie a note. *What's so interesting back there?*

Just want to see if Melissa's here, she writes back. I huff and slip the paper into my Bible. Is that all? Just looking for old gooseneck Melissa?

I sit forward and try to concentrate on the sermon. Then all the people to my right start shifting or standing and I look down to see Melissa coming down the row. Could she sit at the end of the pew? Could she sit in the back of the church? No, she's got to work her way to us because, God Almighty, she is a princess. Her parents sit in the row behind us. Lord, these people have a habit of disturbing the spirit.

Then I see Melissa's shirt, sequined and sparkly—the same one as Lottie's. My back curls into a tight whip as I lean and stare at her.

"Excuse me," she whispers as she tries to pass me. I roll my eyes, then shift my legs, but only a little.

Melissa shakes her head and waits. I don't look at her; I don't move. Don't even think you're sitting between me and Lottie. But then Lottie's family moves down, and Melissa squeezes past me and sits between Lottie and Tootsie. Tootsie beams.

I hope it ain't a sin to be mad in church.

I try to stare straight ahead, but the corner of my eye is picking up all the sparkliness that's happening to my left. Even the diamond chip in Lottie's watch twinkles with light.

I pull the notepaper from my Bible and scribble furiously. *Why is she wearing your shirt?*

Her mom bought them at the mall. Mine was free.

I think she added the last part to make me feel better, like she got the shirt by accident. I pout my lips and slam back against the pew.

Now Melissa hands her a note. Without turning my head, I slide my eyes over the words. Her cursive letters swirl over the paper: *You look great!* Well sure, of course she would think so; they both got on the same shirt. Then I'm hit like a bolt of lightning—she wants to be twins with Lottie.

My body tightens. I clench my teeth. Lottie smiles at her and writes something back. I can't see it.

I scribble my own note and push it into her right hand. *What's she writing about?*

Nothing, she writes back. *Just stuff about her shirt.*

On her left comes Melissa's note. I lean over to get a better view: *You have a really good shape! Did you talk to your mom about—*

"Violet!" Lottie snaps and turns the note over. She looks mad.

Something's going on. Why won't she let me see? I pretend to sit back in the pew, but I use my slow-moving statue skills to spy.

Lottie writes something quick. All I've managed to see is: *and what if she says no?*

"Who says 'no'?" I whisper in her ear.

"Violet!" Lottie says, then clamps her hand over her mouth. Her mom leans forward and frowns at her. Lottie slips the note to Melissa, shifts over to me, and goes, "It's nothing, okay?"

I lean my head toward her. "It's something, or you wouldn't be hiding it."

We sit there, all three of us, facing forward for a minute. Then Melissa slips another note into Lottie's hand. Despite my best efforts, I can't see the words.

I touch Lottie's arm. "Is it about me?" I whisper.

"No! Violet, please." Her eyes plead with me. Is this the privacy she was talking about? From me? My lips press together.

Lottie starts to write again. Melissa takes the paper from her, scribbles, then hands it back. Lottie cups it with her hands and reads it between her fingers. My Lord, what could be so important? I'm tired of this mysterious note. I try to snatch it. Lottie whips the note away from me, and then her mom stretches across Tootsie and Melissa and grips her arm. In a low voice, she says to Lottie, "Stop, or I'll pass my own note across your bottom."

Tears fill Lottie's eyes and pink creeps up her neck and into her face. She slides the note into her Bible and doesn't look at anyone for the rest of the service.

Neither do I, 'cause I'm thinking about how to get ahold of that note, but service lets out before I can develop a plan. If I changed my name today, it would be Suspicious Violet or Mad Violet. Well, maybe not Mad Violet, because sometimes "mad" means crazy, so I'd have to think twice about that. But I only have to think once about Lottie's new name: Benedict Arnold.

14

Yesterday, I was boiling hot mad in church when Melissa and Lottie were passing notes back and forth and Lottie wouldn't even tell me what they were talking about. When church was over, I grabbed Momma off that platform and said, "Come on, let's go." I barely even looked at Lottie when we left.

But later, after Momma and I had gotten a good ways down the road, the Townsends' truck roared by. Mr. Townsend honked the horn and the girls leaned out and shouted, "Violet! Violet!" Lottie hung out the window and waved. "See you in a few!"

Well, my heart swelled up and I waved back and watched their truck tear down their driveway, spinning out a cloud of dust.

"Going to the fish fry?" Momma asked.

"Yep." 'Course I was. I couldn't be mad anymore,

not after the whole Townsend family practically fell out of the truck to make sure I was coming.

"I think I may take a nap, then," Momma said, as if this wasn't the same conversation we had every Sunday.

After she lay down, I got myself ready and ran over to Lottie's.

"Where's Melissa?" I asked Lottie soon as I walked through her back door. Figured I better prepare myself.

Lottie raised her eyebrows and handed me a paring knife for the lemons. "I think Melissa's done with fish fries."

"That's too bad," I said. I didn't mean it, of course, but it seemed like the right thing to say. I made a clean slice through a lemon and it squirted me on the cheek.

"Yep," Lottie said. "Just you and me."

I couldn't help but smile even though I'd just stuck a lemon in my mouth.

So things are right back to normal today. Lottie and I are in her kitchen making crusts for apple pies. I'm pressing out a perfect pastry circle. This is a chore I like, pushing the rolling pin like a steamroller across the dough. I stretch the dough till it's almost breaking. Then I poke two holes in the top half for eyes and a bunch of holes, snowman-style, for a smile.

"Look," I say.

Lottie stops rolling for a second, looks up, and laughs. Setting aside her rolling pin, she pokes some holes in her dough. "Look at mine!"

Her face is even better—she made *X*s for the eyes and a line for the lips, so her dough face is either asleep or drunk. We giggle and ball up our dough to roll it out again.

When I look up, I notice Lottie's got her bathing suit on under her shirt. Yesterday, too. Well, it is hot in here. They don't have air-conditioning either, and the fans are just blowing the hot air around.

"We going swimming later?"

Lottie tilts her head. "What?"

"We going swimming?" I point to her neck where her bikini top is tied. "You got your suit on."

Lottie licks her lips. "Oh, that. Um . . ." She looks down, rolls a little dough, looks back up. "I don't know if there'll be time."

"What do you mean? I'll just run and get my suit after we get these pies in." No big deal.

"Well, I mean, like—" She sets her rolling pin down and looks at me straight on. "Okay, don't be mad, but Melissa invited me over to watch *Paris Heights* with her."

My eyes narrow into slits so thin I can barely see out of them. My cheeks turn into stone.

Her shoulders droop. "Violet!"

"What?" I say and purse my lips.

"She's nice. I don't know why you don't like her."

"I never said that!"

Lottie leans her head. "It kind of shows."

I look away from her so she can't see that I know what she's talking about. "She tries to be so glamorous all the time."

"She thinks you have pretty eyes."

Okay, I do like hearing that. But still, I'm not giving up my best friend for "pretty eyes." I shrug so's Lottie can see I don't care about that.

She heaves a big sigh. "I'm allowed to have other friends, you know. You do."

I lay my perfect pie circle in a pan. I grit my teeth as I roll out the next ball. "No, I don't."

"What do you call Eddie?" She settles a crust and rolls out another ball too. "Half the time you're out doing something with him."

I roll faster, harder. "Eddie doesn't count. He's a

boy. Besides, you don't like doing some of the stuff we do."

We got the crusts in the pans and the tops rolled out. The windows darken as we work.

"Maybe there's stuff I like to do that you don't like to do." She pinches around the crust so the top and bottom'll stay together. "I'm just saying that you have other friends and I don't get mad about it."

It's true. She don't ever get mad when I'm out with Eddie. But like I said, Eddie's a boy. Melissa's trying to get my spot. I try to get the madness out of my face. It's still in my heart, but I don't want Lottie to know that. I just want everything to be like it always is. I grab the apples and a knife and start cutting. "I don't see what's so interesting about *Paris Heights*."

Lottie laughs and grabs an apple. "You've never even seen it."

I am beginning to simmer. She knows Momma don't allow me to watch programs like that. I use my knife like an ax. *Chop. Chop. Chop.* I'm done cutting apples. As we mix the apples with sugar and spices, a long train of thunder rumbles by.

"I wonder if we'll have time to bake these pies," Lottie says.

"Plenty of time," I say. I dump the filling into both pans and we lay the tops on. "That thunder is far away."

Then it booms again.

"I don't know," Lottie says, a worried look on her face. "Sounds like it's getting louder to me."

Thunder drums in the clouds again. Irritation crosses over me. I know what she's getting at. "You just want to hurry up and go to Melissa's."

"No, I don't. I just don't know if there's time for these pies to bake before the storm starts."

"You can't tell when a storm's going to hit? Well, I can tell you." I grab the pies, open the oven, and slide them in. "It ain't hitting now, so these pies are going in." I slam the oven shut. *Paris Heights* will have to wait.

I spin around and look at her. "What do you want to do now?" I ask. "We can't go swimming."

Lottie fingers the ties at her neck. "Let me clean up this mess first." She goes to the sink, looking out the dark window as she runs the water.

A soft light flashes inside the clouds. *One thousand one, one thousand two, one thousand three*—crack!

Lottie turns around. "I think we should turn everything off."

I stand up and cross my arms. "No! That storm is three miles away."

A bright strike flashes through the back windows and I forget to count.

Lottie frowns at me and stomps over to the box fan. "That's it. I'm turning everything off." She twists the knob, crosses her arms, and looks at me.

Static rushes across my scalp and down my arms. All my hairs stand up. I look at Lottie in slow motion and my mouth starts to form her name. Then light races down the kitchen wall and flares out the oven and at the same time—*BOOM!*—a bomb explodes. My ears are deafened. My heart hammers against my chest.

I start crying.

A fire is burning inside the oven. The smoke detectors shriek and Lottie's screaming and I'm screaming too 'cause I don't know what to do— Lord, help me—and then I'm getting up, I'm grabbing Lottie, and we stumble out of there and cross the yard, slipping and falling through the rain till we climb my steps and fall into my house. We hug each other and cry.

Then I remember learning 9-1-1 in school. I let go of her and run to the phone.

"What's your emergency?" the lady asks.

I sob into the phone.

The lady says, "Take a breath and speak clearly. What's your emergency?"

I take one big breath. "My best friend's house just got struck by lightning."

15

My best friend is homeless. Actually, it's worse than that. My best friend and her sisters are staying at Melissa's house.

"It's just temporary," Mrs. Townsend told the girls when everyone was still at our house. By this time, some of the neighbors had come out to see what happened. Including Mrs. Gold.

Mr. and Mrs. Townsend decided to stay in their house so they could work on it. But Lottie, Hannah, Ashley, and Tootsie needed somewhere to stay.

Momma offered right away for them to stay with us, but Mrs. Gold rushed in with her offer, making it sound better. "We have all that room and it's just going to waste. You come," she said, nodding. "We want you to stay with us."

I bet they did. I could just imagine Melissa giving Lottie daily movie-star lessons.

Mrs. Townsend's eyes welled up. "If you're sure it wouldn't be too much of a burden."

"I'm looking forward to a house full of kids. I'm home all day. You can do what you need to do and I'll watch the kids." She looked like she wanted to say more, but she stopped and waited.

I waited too. I couldn't believe this was happening. Momma couldn't top that offer—she *had* to work.

Mrs. Townsend bit her lip. "I don't know what I'm going to do about clothes. Everything in there is soaked."

Mrs. Gold waved her hands and shook her head. "Don't worry about that. We'll shove everything they need into plastic bags. I'll run the wash when we get home."

After that, there was nothing left to say. The two of them went over, filled the bags with clothes, and came back for the girls.

I hug Lottie hard when they leave. "I'm going to miss you," I say, tears streaming down my face.

She's crying too. "I'll miss you, too, Violet." She wipes her eyes and laughs. "But I'll just be down the street. We'll still see each other."

"Yeah," I say, but I don't believe it. Melissa will guard Lottie like a bulldog. There's something else I got to say. It's hard, but if I don't say it, it'll crush me—it's that heavy. "I'm sorry I made you bake those pies."

Lottie's eyes fill. "It wasn't the oven," she says. She leans closer and whispers, "It was the antenna. The firemen said so." She widens her eyes and leans back. "They said it was like a lightning rod."

"Oh, my Lord," I say. That old TV antenna of theirs sticks way up. My heart feels good and terrible at the same time—good 'cause it wasn't my fault, and terrible for feeling good.

It's nighttime when they leave. Momma and me wave till we don't see them no more, then Momma slips her arm around my shoulders and we step into the empty house. In my mind, I replay the lightning and the screaming and 9-1-1 and the taillights of the car I just watched disappear down the road. My breath comes in ragged, and my lips pull back tight. I clench my eyes shut. I turn into Momma's side and push my face into her. For the third time tonight, I'm bawling like a baby.

16

Lottie's house looks normal from the outside. I stare at it real hard as I pass by on my way to Melissa's. It's hard to believe that something that looks the same as it always has is suddenly so different on the inside.

Lord, I can't believe how hot it is today. I swear if Lottie has her suit on, I'm running through the sprinkler with my clothes on, that's how hot I am.

Eddie flies around the bend on his bike, pops a wheelie, and rides it. I can't help but be impressed. He races down the road and skids to a perfect stop right in front of me, causing clouds of dust to puff up around us.

"Don't get me dirty," I say and keep walking. "I'm going somewhere."

He hops off his bike and walks alongside me. "Where you going?"

"Melissa's."

His eyebrows shoot up into a question.

"I been there before," I say. "Besides, Lottie's staying there."

Eddie's jaw drops. "What?"

He doesn't even know about Lottie's house! I describe everything—the explosion, the lightning racing down the wall, and how, if I'd have been touching that oven, I would've been struck down dead, dead, dead.

"Whoa!" Eddie says. "Man!"

I like that he's impressed.

"But why are they staying at Melissa's if the house didn't burn down?" he asks.

"It didn't burn down," I say. "It was burning inside the walls. The firemen had to chop it all open and hose down the wires." I know this 'cause I overheard Mrs. Townsend telling Momma and Mrs. Gold. I remember something else. "The firemen said the antenna was a big lightning rod."

Eddie looks off to the side, and I realize he's picturing that antenna looming over Lottie's house. "Man." He shakes his head. "But you know what they say, Florida's the lightning capital of the United States." He raises his eyebrows. "We're in *lightning alley.*"

I get the shivers hearing him say that.

We walk down a bit, pushing lovebugs out of

our way. Don't ever swat lovebugs. You'll kill them, that's how delicate they are. The sun's burning me flat into the ground. It's so humid, my shirt sticks to my back. I sweep up my hair and hold it up with one hand while we walk.

Eddie looks at me and looks down before looking at me again. "Hey, Violet, you want to—"

"Violet, Violet!" Tootsie runs down Melissa's porch steps and across the walk.

"Tootsie-Tutu!" I yell. I swoop her up and swing her around.

"Do it again!" she says when I put her down. But I grab her hand and go up the walk.

Lottie pops up. "Violet!" She smiles and starts for the steps.

Then I see Melissa's gooseneck pop up. Well, what can you expect? She does live here and all. Her chest heaves with a big sigh when she sees me. That's okay. I don't say hi to her either. Then she looks past me and smiles at Eddie.

Lottie jumps down the stairs and hugs me like she ain't seen me in a year. A good feeling goes through me, and it gets even better when I notice the jealous look on Melissa's face. I'm glad she's not part of this, and I'm glad she knows it.

Lottie leans around me. "Hey, Eddie."

"Hey." He leans forward on his handlebars. "You guys want to go to the cave?" he asks. "We could pick up cups on the way."

I'm about to say yes, a BrainFreeze would sure be good on a day like this, but Lottie speaks up before I do. "Not me. I'm looking at magazines with Melissa."

Eddie turns to me. "Violet, you want to come?"

I'd love to squeeze into that cave and hear that whooshing sound again. And suddenly a root beer BrainFreeze is just what I got a craving for. But when I look at Lottie, her eyes ask me to stay.

"Naw, I think I'm going to stay here for a while."

He doesn't say anything back, just turns his bike around and heads down the road.

"Wait till you see the autographs Melissa's got!" Lottie says as we climb up the porch and sit on the floor by Melissa. Tootsie sits on my lap.

Those stupid letters. "I seen them before," I say. Already, I am regretting not heading down that road with Eddie.

Melissa huffs. "Not all of them." She spreads out a pile of those plastic sheets, talking without looking up. "Walked here with your boyfriend, huh?"

I sneer at her. "He ain't my boyfriend." Then I roll my eyes at Lottie so's she can see how stupid

Melissa is. As if Eddie and I would ever act all googly-eyed and stuff.

"Whatever." Melissa busies herself with her letters. "He looks kind of like this guy," she says, flashing a plastic-encased photo.

I can see the resemblance, dark hair and blue eyes, but I never thought of Eddie as one of those fancy Hollywood types. Eddie is a real person.

Lottie leans over and looks at the picture. "You're right. He does kind of look like that guy."

Oh, my Lord. I can't believe I'm sitting on this porch wasting time over these pictures. My legs drip with sweat and I push Tootsie off my lap. Then I remember about swimming and I look over and see Lottie's bathing suit tied up under her shirt. "You guys want to hook up a sprinkler?" I ask, then turn to Melissa. "Or you got a pool we can fill up?"

Tootsie jumps up and down and claps her hands. "Sprinkler!" She runs into the house. I hear her yelling for her bathing suit, but it comes out as "babing boot."

"I've got makeup on," Melissa says. "We weren't planning on running through the sprinkler." She acts like she's embarrassed I said such a thing.

I look at Lottie. "Why you got your bathing suit on then?"

Lottie's face burns a slow pink. She looks at Melissa. This makes me mad, something secret going on between them.

"What?" I cross my arms.

Melissa sighs. "If you must know, she's in training."

"Training?" I ain't heard nothing about a swim contest. "For what?"

Lottie looks down.

Melissa shakes her head and smirks. "She's in training for a bra. I can't believe you even had to ask. You're so dense."

That last comment stings. Lottie doesn't even raise her head or stick up for me. A hardness covers my heart.

Tootsie flings open the door waving her bathing suit. "I need help!"

I stand up and stop near the top of the porch stairs. "You can put that suit away, Tootsie. They don't want to go swimming. They don't want to go to the cave. They don't want to do anything except look at boring old magazines."

Lottie stands up. She looks hurt.

Good. Now she knows how it feels.

"Are you leaving?" she asks.

Her voice sounds small, but I'm too mad to

care. "If I'm lucky," I say, "I can catch up to Eddie and do something fun."

Melissa jumps to her feet. "Yeah, catch up to Eddie. We all know you have a *crush* on him!"

Lottie's hand flies up to her mouth.

"Do not!" I holler.

"Do too!"

I yell louder. "Do not!"

Melissa waves her hand like she's shooing away a mosquito. "Go on, now. Run to your loverboy." She starts laughing.

"Don't go, Violet, she's just teasing," Lottie says.

I look from Lottie to Melissa. I can't stand the smirk on Melissa's face. "I'm leaving."

I stomp down the stairs, smashing the good feelings I had with every step. I reach the bottom and it only takes a second to realize I must turn left to my house instead of right to where Eddie went.

I don't have a crush on him.

17

"Momma, what made you fall in love with my daddy?" I've come for lunch on an especially good day—Momma's made chocolate cupcakes with peanut butter frosting, special order, but there were two extras. I'm almost finished with mine.

Momma sets her fork down. She's eating her cupcake with a fork so's not to disturb her lipstick. She smiles. "Now why are you asking me that?"

I make the exact opposite of a smile. Some people think that's a frown, but they're wrong. The exact opposite of a smile is an I-don't-care face, like I make now. "Just wondered." I take a bite out of my cupcake.

It works, 'cause she looks past me and I can tell she's looking through the memories in her head. Her face gets all soft and, for a moment, she looks younger. "I'd seen your daddy around church and in school. All us girls knew who he was—"

"How? Was he class president or something important?"

Momma laughs softly. "No, he was never president or anything like that. He just—it was just the way he was."

Well, this is no help at all. "If he wasn't anything important, how'd everyone know who he was?"

"Your daddy played guitar in church. I guess that's how the other boys knew who he was. And us girls, too—he looked just like Elvis Presley up on that platform. He was so good looking, and bashful too. That made us like him even more."

I wrinkle my nose and pull my head back. "You mean you had a crush on him?"

"I think everyone had a crush on your father. Me and my best friend joined the choir just to be near him."

I nearly fall off my chair hearing that. "You started singing so's you could be near a boy?"

Momma laughs. "Oh, yes! I just wanted to be near him, anything just to be with him. I couldn't believe it when the pastor put us up front to sing together." Momma's eyes are wet with sad-happy tears. "He said we had perfect harmony."

"So did everyone start teasing you 'bout you and daddy?"

"Actually," Momma says, "I think they were a little jealous." Momma's face begins to focus and I can almost see the memory evaporating like a cloud. "Why?" she asks. "Are people teasing you 'bout someone?"

I quickly put on the I-don't-care face, but it's too late. I can tell by the way she waits on my answer she's seen my real face.

"Kind of," I say. I shrug. I don't want this to be a big deal. "They're teasing me about Eddie. Melissa thinks he's cute."

"He is a nice-looking boy."

I rise halfway out of my seat. "I don't have a crush on him!"

Momma looks startled. "I didn't say you did."

"Yeah, but you said he's a nice-looking boy."

"I didn't mean anything by it."

"Yes, you did," I say and scoot my chair back. "You think I have a crush on him just like they do."

Momma looks confused. "Violet—"

"Well, you're wrong." I slam my chair into the table.

I know she can't follow me 'cause she's still on the clock. The air conditioner hits me as I walk through the electric doors, the last breath of cool air before I go into the heat.

18

Lottie's getting especially hard to track down these days. I walked all the way to Melissa's only to find out that Lottie was at her own home. At least I didn't run into old gooseneck herself.

Mr. Townsend is carrying lumber from his truck when I come up the drive. "Hey, Vi."

"Hey." I feel a couple of sprinkles. Seems too early for rain. "Mrs. Gold said Lottie was here."

He stacks the lumber on a pile by the porch, takes off his baseball cap, and wipes his forehead with his arm, which I can see is scraped up from all his work. "She went to the store with her mother. She'll be right back." He points to a far corner of the porch. "You can wait with Melissa if you want."

A raindrop plops right into my eye as I look at her, sitting like a cat on the banister.

She spreads out a fake smile while saying

something different with her eyes. I fake-smile back. I wish I had fangs. Mr. Townsend gets back to his work, not even knowing the darts that have just been thrown right in front of him. I ain't sitting on the porch with her. I settle on the steps.

Finally, their car crunches up the driveway. Lottie bursts out practically before Mrs. Townsend's even got the engine off. Her face is shining and she looks different. Same haircut, so it's not that. Shirt looks different, but, yeah, I've seen it before.

"Hey, hey, hey!" Mrs. Townsend yells after her. "How about helping with these bags?"

Lottie shakes her fists in front of her so's only I can see. I pop up from the stairs and go with her for the bags. Rain comes down a little harder. Melissa runs from the porch to help and we all dash inside.

I ain't been inside this house since the lightning strike. I almost drop my bags when I glance around the kitchen. Whole sections of walls have been tore into. I can see straight to the inside bones and wires of the house. My eyes well up with tears. There's scorch marks everywhere.

Even though Mr. and Mrs. Townsend have been cleaning up, chunks of drywall litter the floor.

I smell mildew and charred wood. I set the bags down and drift into the living room. Lottie and Melissa follow. The living room's been hacked up too, and the carpet feels squishy.

"Oh, my gosh," Melissa murmurs.

"Is it like this upstairs?" I whisper to Lottie.

She nods.

I lean on the couch but lift myself away quickly. "It's wet."

Lottie shrugs. "They had to spray."

The living room is as far as I can go. I don't want to see no more of this.

When we go back into the kitchen, Mr. and Mrs. Townsend are real quiet. She's staring straight at him. "What do they say?"

He doesn't answer. His eyebrows lower as he keeps reading a letter.

"What's wrong?" By the way her voice cracks, I can tell that letter's got bad news in it.

He looks at her like there's no one else in the room. "Insurance isn't going to pay," he says. "They say we've been delinquent."

"We're criminals?" Lottie says.

"Means late," I say. "Delinquent also means late."

Mrs. Townsend's face goes slack, and she leans against the counter.

Mr. Townsend wipes his face with his hand and closes his eyes for a second.

Fear rises in me.

Lottie steps closer. "So? What does that mean?"

Mr. Townsend stares at Mrs. Townsend. "We don't have the money to fix everything." He swallows hard. "We might have to sell."

My body goes rigid. My heart pounds in my ears. "Sell?" My voice comes out quiet. "But you live here."

"You dummy," Melissa says and snatches my arm. "They can't live here if they can't fix it."

Lottie clenches her teeth and turns on us. Her eyes glitter. "Shut up! Just shut up, okay?"

I feel like I just been slapped. Tears well up in my eyes.

Lottie says, "I'm sorry, you guys, okay? I just—"

Mrs. Townsend turns to us. Her eyes are moist and her voice cracks when she speaks. "Girls, this isn't a good time right now." She rubs her eyes. "Maybe you should go home."

I stumble down Lottie's steps like a blind person, my eyes are so blurry with tears. It's raining good now, but no thunder or lightning.

Melissa blocks my path and leans into me. "This is your fault," she hisses. I imagine horns on top of her head.

"No, it's not," I say. "It was the antenna! Lottie said so herself." I wipe the rain from my cheeks.

Putting her hands on her hips, she gets in my face and says, "Of course she said that. She doesn't want you to feel bad."

It wasn't my fault. I would die if it were my fault. "Florida's the lightning capital of the United States," I shout. "Eddie told me that."

She smirks. "Oh, yeah—your loverboy."

I can't take no more of it. I clench my teeth and push her.

She trips backward. Her eyes go wide open, then she gets her balance back and her meanness too. "Are you going to pull my hair now?"

My feelings are swirling around and I can't fight good right now. "Shut up!"

She snorts. "Nice comeback. What else did you learn on the playground?"

It's too much. I lunge at her, but she's onto me this time and slips out of the way. Without a target to hit, my body swings out of balance, my arms spin like windmills, and my legs tangle. I fall in a heap.

When I get up, Melissa has a superior look on her face. On a good day, I could wipe that look off in ten seconds, maybe nine. But this ain't a good day. I get up, brush myself off, and stalk past her through the rain to my house.

Usually, I like sun showers, but I can't see no rainbow in this one.

19

I'm on my porch, two doormats away from the fattest dragonfly I've ever seen. I don't even know what I'll do if I catch him.

"Violet!" Lottie's voice.

At first, I flick my eyes up without moving, but then I see Melissa with her, so I straighten up and act like I was just waiting for them to come down the road. The dragonfly takes off. My shoulders slump and I plop down on our porch swing.

They get to my front walk and climb up the porch steps.

"What were you doing?" Melissa asks snidely.

"What were you doing?" I ask back in the same voice.

She huffs and rolls her eyes.

Lottie sits on the swing beside me. There's enough room for Melissa, but she don't sit down. Lottie says, "We're going to search for shells by the bridge. Want to come?"

'Course I do. "Let me just close up the house." I wonder if Lottie had to ask special permission from Melissa to invite me. Suddenly, I'm glad I let Melissa come to the cave with us that day.

I go in, and as soon as the door swings shut, I hear Melissa talking. She don't know the windows are open. I hide real quick behind the sheer drapes in case anything gets said I should know about. They can't see me, but I can see Melissa's face and the back of Lottie's head.

"Do you think she'll find out today?" Melissa asks.

Ooh, I'm so glad I'm catching this secret.

Lottie waits for a second before answering. It must be something important.

"No, because Chad is still in a coma, remember?"

What? Who's Chad? I know everyone Lottie knows, and I sure haven't heard about no Chad in a coma.

"Oh, yeah," Melissa says. "I can't believe they ended the program like that. I can't wait to see what happens today!"

Oh, my Lord, they're talking about that stupid *Paris Heights*. I'm about to walk away when Lottie changes the subject.

"I still feel bad about your mom last night. I know she was trying to help." Lottie tucks her hair behind her ear. "It's just that Tootsie's only three, and she's used to being at home with our mom." Lottie's voice crumbles on that last part.

"Yeah, that's what my mom said too." Melissa sighs. "Poor Tootsie! I've never seen anyone cry like that before, and every night! My mom thinks she'll be all right, though; she'll get used to being at our house."

I try to picture Tootsie in Melissa's house, but I can't do it. I can only imagine her in her and Lottie's room—Tootsie-Tutu and her dolls, Tootsie and me and Purple Eyebrows. It crushes me to think of Tootsie crying every night. My eyes get big and wet but I don't blink.

I hear a ragged breath and when I look back out, Lottie's head is bent. Melissa slips onto the swing next to Lottie and puts her arm around her. "Don't cry, Lottie," she says. "Your dad will work it out. He's on the phone with the insurance people every day."

"I know," Lottie says. "But . . ."

She don't say nothing else. Then they just sit there, swinging.

My throat aches something awful. I stand there,

not because I am a slow-moving statue, but because a heaviness has filled me up. Waves of sadness wash over me. I quietly move away from the living room and close up the other rooms.

When I walk back up to the front, I make a lot of noise; I don't want to hear anything else I'm not supposed to. But when I push on the front window, it don't budge. It's stuck open. Gritting my teeth, I stand on my tiptoes and haul the window down with all my might. *Blam!* Melissa startles at the noise, but I don't get no pleasure out of it, that's how bad I'm feeling.

I put on my fake-happy face when I step out. I haven't had much practice with this one 'cause I usually don't have to fake this face, but it's been an awful hard summer. As we walk, Lottie talks more about her dad yelling on the phone and Tootsie crying every time Mr. and Mrs. Townsend leave; then we start talking about school and I find out me and Lottie won't even be in class together.

As we cut into the woods, we see Eddie.

"Eddie!" I shout. Then I remember what Melissa said about Eddie and me, and I look at her real quick. But she's not looking at me; she's looking at him, and her face has gone all soft.

"Hey, Violet!" He throws a stick into the woods

and meets us on the path. "Hey," he says to Lottie and Melissa. Even though Melissa has teased me about him, I can't help but be pleased that mine is the only name he actually says.

"We're going to look for shells by the bridge," Lottie says. "Want to come?"

"Sure. Might see Alfred today."

Before I can chime in to correct the name, Melissa says, "Who's Alfred?"

Eddie looks at her wide-eyed. "You ain't heard of Alfred?"

Melissa shakes her head. She listens carefully.

"Alfred is the biggest alligator we've spotted," he says. I notice he don't mention we ain't seen *Allie* since last year.

"Alligator!" Melissa says. By the lift of her voice, I can't tell if she's excited or scared, but I choose scared for her.

I walk up and stand by Eddie. "No big deal," I say.

Melissa's look of awe radiates. "You mean you saw it too?"

I shrug one shoulder. "Yeah."

She stares at us, then squints and shakes her head. "No way!"

"It's true," Lottie says. "Even though I didn't see it."

Melissa shakes her head. "How could alligators live here? There's houses around here."

"Well, they don't live in houses," I say.

Eddie shoots me a grin. I snicker too, 'cause that was pretty funny.

❦ ❦ ❦

We scratch the dirt with sticks, looking for shells. I've found two white ones, but I could find those anywhere. I throw them into the river, hear them plunk. I'm hoping to find something different.

Melissa's looking for shells like the rest of us, but she's careful not to get her fingers or her clothes dirty. How she expects to find anything scratching so dainty-like is beyond me. Straightening up, she walks over to Lottie. Her eye makeup has sweated into the corners of her eyes.

"Do like this," Lottie says, making a motion with her fingers. It's official, then; they're really friends now. But I remind myself that Lottie dragged Melissa all the way to my house, passing these very woods just to come get me. That has to mean something.

Melissa digs the black goop from the inside corners of her eyes. "Are you sure there are shells here?" she asks. "We're not even by the ocean."

"There's shells everywhere," I say. "Even mounds built out of shells."

Melissa just looks at me. "Well, if this river flows down to the ocean, I don't see how shells could be here."

"Shows how much you know," I say. I scoop a little brown shell from the dirt and hold it up for her inspection. "Besides," I say, "this river doesn't flow south—it flows north."

Melissa puts her hands on her hips. "All rivers flow south."

Lottie waves her stick. "Actually, this one does flow north. We learned it in school."

Melissa looks like she doesn't believe her. She starts to lean against a tree, thinks better of it, and just stands there. She drops her stick. "We're not going to find anything."

"Who's crossing this bridge with me?" Eddie calls out. He's halfway there.

Melissa almost pops off the ground. "I'll do it!"

He looks at her, then over to me. "Violet? You coming?"

I look down to my shell digging. "Can't," I yell back. "I think I found a tiny shell mound."

"I'll still go," Melissa says.

Eddie looks at her and shakes his head. "I guess

we came for shells anyway." He trudges back, passes her, and crouches next to me.

The dead branches of a tree near the river's edge look like they might work better than the stick I already have. I walk over and snap one off, and something catches my eye, something floating in the water that wasn't there before.

My breath comes out in puffs. My legs are paralyzed. A forehead floats through the river, two yellow eyes that pretend not to see me. Floating close so gently, he don't even make a ripple. Then his ridgy back breaks through the surface. I scream and stumble back.

Everyone scrambles to me. They don't see him right away. "What? What?" they're all yelling. I raise my hand and point to the alligator gliding silently toward us.

My face drains.

"It's him!" Eddie shouts. "It's Alfred!"

Alligators run up to thirty-five miles per hour. They got eighty teeth. If they catch you, they drag you into the water and hurl you into the death roll.

Lottie grabs my arm. "Let's go!"

I can't move. She shakes me, but I can't move.

"Let's go!" She shakes me harder.

I snap out of it and turn, running behind her.

Melissa's already running down the path in front of us.

"Where you going?" Eddie yells from the riverbank. "It might be another year before we see him again!"

I don't answer. I'm too busy escaping. Another year would be okay with me.

20

Lord Almighty, I'm about to collapse by the time we run up to Melissa's porch. My heart is pounding harder than a jackhammer and I'm wheezing to catch my breath. Sinking to the porch floor, I glance at Lottie and Melissa. Their faces are red, and they're breathing hard too.

The screen door pops open and Mrs. Gold steps out. "I thought I heard a bunch of elephants jumping on the porch!"

Melissa looks at her mom. She speaks between breaths. "Mom! You wouldn't believe it! An alligator!"

Mrs. Gold's smile drops and her eyebrows draw close together. "What?"

"In the river—we saw an alligator in the river!"

Mrs. Gold looks at Lottie and me. "Is that true? Are you sure it wasn't a log?"

"No, ma'am," I say. "That was a true alligator. An eight-footer, I'd say."

Melissa nods.

Mrs. Gold frowns and puts her hands on her hips. "If there was really an alligator, I want you to stay away from that river." She tips her head at Melissa. "You got me?"

"Don't worry about that," Melissa says. "I have no problem staying away from alligators."

Lottie and me laugh a little. Well, you got to figure a city girl isn't going to appreciate seeing your wildlife unless she's seeing it on TV. Melissa's mom tells us to come on in and she's got lemonade for us. I must admit after all that running around, the air-conditioning and ice-cold lemonade are just what I need.

¥ ¥ ¥

When we get inside, Tootsie wraps me in a big hug, and Hannah and Ashley run into the kitchen from the living room. I can hear people laughing on the TV. The girls make us tell the alligator story a hundred times while we drink our lemonade and eat cookies. The cookies are from Parker's, and I feel good knowing that I'm eating something made by my own momma's hands. I can't believe it, but I'm actually enjoying myself in Melissa's house.

Lottie's sisters run back to the living room,

then Melissa glances at the clock. "It's almost time for *Paris Heights*," she says. She looks at me. "It's really not that bad. Are you sure you're not allowed to watch it?"

I shake my head. "I'm not allowed to watch soap operas or anything like that." This is like a commandment, so I never break it, unless Momma makes a special exception, like when I watched Miss America last year with Lottie.

Melissa sighs.

I get up to leave, but Lottie says, "Couldn't we just miss it this one time?" She gestures toward the living room. "Besides, the girls are already watching the TV. We could do something fun without them bothering us."

Melissa thinks on this. "Okay," she says. We follow her upstairs to her room. "Let's do makeovers!"

Lottie squeals and claps her hands.

Apparently, the first step of a makeover is to cleanse your face. This is just what Melissa says. She doesn't say, "Wash your face," like a normal person; she says, "Cleanse your face." Then she will pick one of us to make over. So after our faces are cleansed, she studies me and Lottie, stands back, and nods. "Okay. Violet, we're going to make you over."

My eyebrows scrunch up. "What?" I don't want

no makeover; I'm used to the way I am. "Uh-uh," I say. "Do Lottie."

Melissa leans in real close to my face. I pull my head back. Standing up, she says, "You've got pretty eyes." So it's true; she really did say that before. "But you need to bring them out."

"I don't know...."

Lottie claps her hands and bounces on the bed. "Come on, Violet, it'll be fun!"

I look at them looking at me, and I decide that since Melissa's giving up her soap opera, I could do this little thing for her. I sigh loudly and say, "All right."

Melissa stands to the side of me and holds my head straight, facing her mirror. "Now take a good look," she says. "This is the before picture." The look she puts on her face reminds me of the look she had at the fish fry. I don't think my before face is so bad. I stare at myself in the mirror. I look like me.

"And now"—she turns me around—"I will transform you to the full power of your beauty." She grabs a magazine off her dresser and flips till she finds what she's looking for. "Makeup artist for the stars! I'll do exactly what he says." She leans right into me. "You'll look like a movie star!"

She starts by rubbing skin-colored cream all over my face. "This is step number one: foundation." She's rubbing and patting and it's kind of relaxing. Lottie watches like this is something she should know, like she should be taking notes.

Getting transformed to the full power of my beauty takes a long time. I decide to liven up this conversation. "Can you believe that alligator?"

"Yeah, eight-footer!" Melissa says.

I laugh. "How would you know? I ain't ever seen someone run so fast before."

Melissa swats my head. "I heard your feet running behind me."

I sit up straighter. "Lottie wanted me to run, right, Lottie?"

"Well, yeah, but—"

"But nothing," I say. "I would have stayed there with Eddie 'cept I had to make sure you all made it out okay."

Melissa stops painting me for a moment and leans back. "Oh, really?"

I fold my arms. "Yep."

Now she takes a tiny paintbrush and strokes it over and under my eyes. "I still can't believe we saw a real, live alligator! Wait till I tell my friends in Detroit!" She gets out some blue eye shadow.

God Almighty. "Are you almost done?"

Melissa gives me a snooty look. "I am following the steps precisely. If you'd quit moving around so much, we'd get done sooner."

"It's looking really good," Lottie says. I feel like a project they're both hoping to fix.

Melissa outlines my lips and colors them in, just like my lips were a picture and she has to stay in the lines. Then she powders me up. She stands back. "Done," she says. Lottie and her stare at me.

"Oh, my gosh," Lottie says. "She looks beautiful." The way she says that, it's like I'm not even here.

"Yes, it turned out great."

I don't like being called "it." I start to climb off the bed, but Melissa grabs me by the shoulders. "Wait!" She settles me back into position. "We have to do the before and after."

Okay, I don't even know what she's talking about, but I go along with it just so this whole thing can be over.

"Remember what the before picture looked like?" she asks.

I roll my eyes. 'Course I do—it's the face I look at every day in my own mirror.

"This," she says dramatically while turning me around, "is the after picture."

I can't hardly believe my eyes. I can't hardly see them for one thing, there's so much blue eye shadow on them. My face looks like a cupcake—frosted and colorful. "I don't like it."

I raise my hand to wipe some of it off, but Lottie grabs my arm. "Violet, you look so pretty. You look . . . sophisticated."

Something in her voice tells me this is true. I stare hard at the face looking back at me. Momma wears lipstick, and my own lips look like a blossom, so full and red. My blue eyes are even bluer with my lids covered in eye shadow. Even my cheeks have been highlighted with a rosy color.

Melissa stares at me. "You look like a knockout!"

"We are so ready for junior high!" Lottie says.

Melissa and Lottie beam at me. I glance at myself again. My face is shiny and brilliant. I don't look like your regular girl walking down the street. I look like . . . like . . . *God Almighty!* I look like a movie star! I can hardly turn from my reflection, it's so different from my normal self. Lottie and Melissa stare at me in the mirror. Suddenly, my legs feel like they got to get moving; I can't stand all this sitting around and I can't stand them looking at me with their goofy grins. "I got to go," I say. "Momma'll be home soon."

Mrs. Gold stops me as they walk me out. She lays a hand on her chest. "Violet! I almost didn't recognize you! You look beautiful!"

My face reddens, but I doubt anyone can tell through the makeup.

Melissa and Lottie see me off, waving to me from the porch like they're the parents and I'm the kid they're sending off. I run down the road till I think they can't see me no more.

After I come around the bend, I hear Eddie behind me.

"Violet! You should have stayed!" he yells.

I don't turn around, not yet.

"I saw his teeth!" Eddie's running pounds on the dirt. "Hey, did you hear what I said?"

I wait till he's right behind me. Then I turn around and hit him with the full power of my beauty.

He jerks his head back. His lips curl and his eyes narrow. He looks like he's going to puke, but he just stands there, staring.

Heat stings my face. I spin around and race to my house.

"No, Violet, I didn't mean anything!"

He's yelling and running and catching up, but I'm already at my door, slamming it behind me. I rush to the bathroom and shut myself in. He's banging on the front door, but I ignore him.

I grab the edge of the sink and pull myself up. I can't believe I let Melissa do this to me. And I can't believe Lottie's under her spell. Well, I'm not. I see now what I really look like. Not a movie star. Not a celebrity.

I look like a clown.

Shaky black lines circle my eyes, and blue is smudged from my eyelids to my eyebrows. My lips look like tomato halves. My cheeks are slashed with red. This is not who I am. This is Melissa's idea of who I am.

I grab a wash rag and scrub the new face off. The makeup colors stain the rag. I scrub my skin till it's red and raw and even then it's not enough. I practically have to scrape the makeup off with my fingernails. And I do, layer by layer, until I get back to the old me. The real me.

21

Later that night, Momma and I are sitting in the living room reading when the phone rings. I'm closer, so I go into the kitchen and pick up.

"Violet!" It's Lottie. She don't normally call at night, so immediately I wonder what's going on.

"Hey, Lottie." Then I wait to hear the big story.

But all she says is, "Did your mom like your makeover?"

I screw my face up. I know she can't see me, but I can't help it. "That was clown makeup," I say. "I scrubbed it off as soon as I got home."

"But you looked so good!" She sounds disappointed. "I myself am planning to wear lip gloss when junior high starts."

I sigh heavily. "Is that all you called to talk about? Makeup?"

"I just called to say hi." Her voice sounds small.

Lord, I didn't mean to hurt her feelings. I'm just sick of all this makeover business. But I don't want

Lottie to feel bad, so I try to think of something to say to make her feel better.

She beats me to it. "I forgot to tell you something." When she speaks again, I can tell she's got her hand over the mouthpiece 'cause her voice sounds close and loud. "I got a bra!"

"You what?" I shout. Then I remember Momma's in the next room. I cup my hand over the phone too. "What?"

"The other day, me and my mom."

I don't know what to say. Lottie is acting like this is something to celebrate. I try to think of something encouraging to say, but all I come up with is "Well, if that's what you want."

"Come on, Violet." When I don't answer, she says, "We're almost in junior high, and—"

I cut her off right there. "Junior high or not, I ain't wearing that clown makeup or acting all googly-eyed over boys like Melissa does, and I'm not interested in your bra. Just count me out."

"It's not just that," she says. "There's other stuff."

"Like what?"

"Like . . . since I'm wearing a bra and since I'm getting older, I need more privacy. I need my own room."

I huff into the phone. "Nothing's wrong with

your room. Why're you trying to change everything?"

"I'm not trying! Everything's changing anyway."

I glance through the window at her house,
which she is no longer in. "Lottie—"

"That's another thing!" she says. "I'm tired of
that name. We're going to junior high—I don't
want to be called by a name my sisters made up
because they couldn't pronounce things right."

"But that's your name."

"No, it's not. My name's Charlotte. And that's
the name I want to start using." She pauses. "Don't
you think it sounds elegant?"

"It sounds like a spider," I say. Lottie's not tough
like me. The older junior high kids will call her spider legs or black widow or say her best friend is a
pig, and then I'll have to punch someone. "Your
name's Lottie."

"It just sounds so old-fashioned."

I shake my head. I know just where this is coming from. "Melissa told you that!"

"No, she didn't!"

I'll eat gator tail if that don't sound like Melissa.
"Are you sure? 'Cause that's just how she talks—*no
offense*."

Now Lottie sounds mad. "I only wanted to tell

you some things, but you're always arguing with me. You're not always right, you know."

I'm shocked. I want to say, *I'm not always arguing with you,* but that would be arguing with her. I am silent. I know I'm not always right 'cause I'm looking through the window at a house that's had the guts ripped right out of it.

Lottie huffs into the phone. "If you don't have anything to say, I guess I'm going to hang up now."

I don't have anything to say. We say good-bye to each other, but I stay on the line until I hear her click off.

"I'm sorry," I whisper.

22

I sit in the kitchen chair long after hanging up with Lottie. I can't believe she wants to change her name. I don't care if that's what they named her; no one has ever called her "Charlotte," not even when she's in trouble. Now she wants to use her fancy name, move out of her room, and other things I don't even want to think about.

She's forgotten who she is.

I prop my elbow on the table and lean my head on my hand. I got to think. I got to think hard. I can't help but blame Melissa for this. If Lottie wasn't staying there, Melissa wouldn't be filling her head with these ideas. God Almighty, I got to get her out of there.

I think about asking her to spend the night, but there's two problems with that: number one, that would fix things for only one night. Number two, I'd probably have to invite Melissa.

I grab a pen out of the holder by the phone and twiddle it.

Momma comes in, pours herself a cup of coffee, and stops beside me. "What're you doing, honey?"

I slump onto my other elbow. "Thinking."

" 'Bout what?"

" 'Bout Lottie."

Momma lets out a long sigh. "I know," she says, clutching her coffee cup with both hands. "It's a terrible thing."

I look at her. Which terrible thing is she talking about? Lord knows there's so many, it's hard to pick just one. I'm fretting over that antenna and how it attracted the lightning, but still I shouldn't have made Lottie bake those pies. I'm thinking on Lottie staying at Melissa's and what if they become better friends than me and Lottie, but I'd rather be her second best friend than have her move away. And on top of that, on top of all of that, Melissa's got me so's I have to think twice about Eddie every time I see him.

Everything normal is slipping away. Don't tell me not to worry. How can I not worry with this mishmash of troubles?

My chest heaves with a long sigh. I got to pick

one thing to stew over and right now, that's Lottie and her family.

"What are they going to do, Momma?" My eyes get wet as I wait for her answer, but I don't let myself cry.

She sits down and puts her hand on top of mine. She shakes her head. "I don't know."

My heart twists when she says that. When something's fixable, grown-ups say hopeful things like, "It'll be okay," or "Don't you worry yourself over that," but when a grown-up says "I don't know," you got yourself something to worry about. I hang my head. "What can I do?"

Momma reaches over and rubs my shoulders before getting up. "You can pray for them," she says. She pats me on the back and leaves the room.

I sit there, holding the pen. *Oh, Lord,* I say. Not out loud, 'cause He can hear you when you're talking just in your mind. But I don't get no further than that. I don't know what to ask Him to do.

Then it comes to me. Mr. Townsend's writing letters, but no one's writing back. *He doesn't know Melissa's secret.* I grab a pad of paper and start a letter to our newspaper. I know they help people, 'cause they always got those funds going at Christmas and during hurricane season for people in need.

When I grab the newspaper, it falls open to *Today's Word: jubilant,* which means joyful, full of happiness. I tear *jubilant* out and add it to my word collection. Even though I am the exact opposite of jubilant, I can see it's a good word. It sounds like candy, something colorful and sweet you can chew on for a long time.

Flipping around the newspaper, I find the place they list the names of the writers. One man's name is on top. I figure he's the most important person at the paper, so I address my letter to him and write the first sentence: *My best friend's house got struck by lightning and they are people in need.*

I describe Lottie's family and how they are all split up right now and how they can't possibly move because that would be the worst thing in the world. Describing the lightning's easy; describing everything else is harder. I use my best handwriting.

I look the letter over real good. Only one thing's missing now. I dash out of the kitchen and into the dining room where Momma keeps my school picture in a frame. Sliding it out carefully, I run back and seal my picture and my letter in an envelope. Tomorrow morning, I will mail it.

23

I am inside the cave, listening. The river bubbles nearby. A heron cackles as he flies over. Then the breeze rustles through the trees; that's my favorite part because of the hollow sound it makes inside the cave.

I'm here because I'm thinking. School is fixing to start in a few weeks. I make a list in my head of the good things and a list of the bad things. Good things: riding the bus—I never done that before. Sharing a locker—me and Lottie will be locker-mates and we're going to put up one of those little chalkboards inside and write each other notes. I've already thought of a few notes to leave, like "TTFN," which is a way of saying "Ta-ta for now," and "TGIF," which means "Thank God it's Friday." Another good thing is they have biology class with microscopes and everything. I heard they go out to the pond and put drops of water under the microscope and you see all these wormy things swimming around in there, except, of course, you'd never see them with your own eyes—it takes a special lens to see things that small.

Bad things: you don't stay in the same room all day; you have to go to different classrooms every hour when a bell rings. I worry about getting lost. Or being late. Taking showers after gym class, definitely bad—I do not want to be naked at school. But the worst thing is not having Lottie in my homeroom. We ain't got our schedules yet, so I don't know if she'll be in any of my other classes. I decide the second worst thing would be if we don't have the same lunch hour.

Footsteps crunching over leaves stop my thinking. My heart pounds fast as the sound gets closer. I move deeper into the cave. The footsteps are coming right to me! If only I had a stick. I press against the inside wall of the tree and my heart beats in my throat. My eyes widen.

The cave is suddenly dark as someone squeezes into it. The intruder don't see me at first, and I can't see who it is, it's so dark. I scream as loud as I can. Eddie bolts against the doorway, ramming his shoulder, and he's trying to escape, but I'm grabbing his shirt and trying not to laugh too hard.

"Violet!" he says. He almost sounds mad. "You

trying to give me a heart attack and make me deaf at the same time?"

"I didn't know it was you!" I say. I let go of his shirt.

We squeeze out of the tree and lean against it. "So what were you thinking about in there?" he asks. He knows me, knows the cave is good for that sort of thing.

"School. Who's your teacher?"

When he tells me, I don't recognize the name. So Eddie won't be in my class either. I sigh.

Eddie clears his throat. "You sure looked different the other day." He steals a glance at me and looks away real quick.

My face reddens. I am humiliated thinking about that clown makeup. But I say, "Don't you know anything about makeovers?" He don't have no sisters, so I'm guessing the answer is no.

He shrugs.

I lift my chin in a superior way. "Well, that shows what you know, because Melissa gave me a makeover in case it was a look I'd like to use in junior high." I look at him. "Everyone else liked it." I don't mention what I thought of it.

He nods, doesn't say anything.

I've just lied to him. Everything I said was true,

but there's something dishonest about it. I feel it making a gap between us. We stand in silence. After a few minutes, the woods darken and we look up to see purple-black clouds taking over the sky.

I look at Eddie. "We better get out of here." I ain't taking chances anymore. We run all the way to the edge of the woods, and the first sprinkles hit as we jog onto the dirt road. We're on dangerous ground still—the road is lined with trees. We keep running and when he gets to his turnoff, he runs down the street, making the gap between us wider and wider.

24

Me and Lottie are sitting on her steps with a real-life reporter from the newspaper.

He called this morning after Momma left for work. "Mrs. Raines, please?" he'd said.

"She ain't here." I didn't offer to take a message, 'cause some people just talk and talk and do they think I'm a secretary? I can't write that fast.

"Is this Violet Raines?"

Never identify yourself over the phone. Then I jerk my head—I wasn't supposed to say Momma wasn't home either.

"Actually," I said, "Mrs. Raines is here, but she's taking a shower."

Then he said his name and that he was a reporter from the newspaper and how he got this letter about a tragic incident, that's what he called it, and he wanted to come talk with everyone involved. Today.

"Today?" I shouted. I got that man's number,

called Momma at work, and now here we sit, me and Lottie, the ones involved in the tragic incident.

Except I must admit I don't feel tragic at all. Momma's here, Lottie's whole family's here, and everyone's happy. Even Melissa being here with her momma don't spoil it for me.

First off, he asks each of us to describe in our own words what happened. We interrupt each other a lot, adding details and parts the other one forgot. He laughs. "You girls are like sisters, the way you finish each other's sentences."

We look at each other and giggle. At the same time, I say, "We practically are!" and Lottie says, "Violet practically lives at our house!" and then we laugh some more.

I like how he writes down every little thing we say, like it's so important. The photographer comes over and takes a few pictures of us. Melissa's watching from the side. She wants to be in the picture so bad, I just know it. Well, this is just for those who were involved in the tragic incident, and that is not her.

"Oh, I just want to get one thing right," the reporter says. He looks at Lottie. "Your name, 'Lottie'—is that with an 'i' or a 'y' at the end?"

"Actually, it's—" I start to correct him, but Lottie talks over me.

"Actually, I have a question," she says. "If something's in the paper, does that mean it's the truth? Like that's the way things really are?"

The reporter nods. "We'd get in big trouble if we didn't get things right."

"Okay, then." She takes a big breath. "My name is Char."

I turn so quick I almost snap my neck. "*Char?* Where'd you get that from?"

Lottie's face gets pink, but she keeps her eyes on the reporter. "It's short for Charlotte," she tells him. "C-h-a-r."

Char. It's so pretty. Only one thing: "Did Melissa make that up for you?"

"No." She jerks her head at me. "I came up with it myself."

In that case, "I love it," I say.

"Me too!" Melissa says from the steps. "It sounds like a celebrity name." She waves her hand as if Lottie's new name was on a marquee. "Char!"

"Short for 'Charlotte,'" Lottie says again.

The reporter writes it down. Then he smiles at Melissa. "Okay, Melissa, let's get your story."

I leap up. "She wasn't even there!"

"Violet!" Lottie says as if I'm acting foolish. Melissa swings around the banister and sits on the other side of her. That girl moves just like a cat.

The reporter says, "We want folks to know about the good neighbors around here."

"Thank you," Melissa purrs.

I sit back down 'cause I got to hear what she says. It's all true, how Lottie's family is staying over there, but oh, my Lord, she makes herself out to be an angel, and she really doesn't have anything to do with this. The more I listen, the more my lips pout and my eyes become slits.

Flash! The photographer takes our picture. "One more," he says. I'm so mad at Melissa horning in on mine and Lottie's tragic incident, I don't even make my fake-happy face. I let the real me show through.

25

As soon as the talking was done, the excitement around here cleared out faster than church on Super Bowl Sunday. Momma went back to work and Mrs. Gold went home. Hannah and Ashley ran out back and climbed the big oak. I could already see things getting back to the way I liked them.

The Home Sweet Home people came by right before the newspaper reporter left. They're the people who help rebuild houses for people in need, like when all them hurricanes and tornadoes came through a few years back. I overheard them—they're going to fix everything, even turn Mrs. Townsend's sewing room into a bedroom for Lottie. Mr. and Mrs. Townsend walked around the place like they were newlyweds, hugging and kissing; they even hugged and kissed me. Said it was all my doing, and they were just so thankful for it.

It did my heart good to hear that.

With all that hugging and kissing, I lost track of

Lottie. Now I'm stuck on the porch with my most un-favorite person in the whole entire universe.

Melissa swings around the banister. "Ooh, here comes your boyfriend."

Eddie's flying down the road on his bike. "He's not my boyfriend," I snap. I'm sick to death of her teasing me about him.

"A little touchy, huh?" She flashes a smug grin at me.

Eddie turns down the driveway and skids to a stop. He looks cool doing it, but I can't let my feelings show because Melissa would bother me to no end over it.

"Hey," he says.

"Hey, Eddie," I say.

"Hi, Eddie." Melissa bounces down the steps. "Have you heard? Char and Violet and I are going to be in the newspaper! Isn't that exciting?"

"Char?" He looks confused. "Who's Char?"

'Course he don't know who that is. Melissa's just saying it 'cause she wants to act like her and Lottie are the real best friends.

"That's Lottie's new name—Char," I say to him nicely. I won't let Melissa make a fool out of him.

"Short for Charlotte," Melissa says. "Isn't it cool?"

"I love it," I say, staking my claim. I *was* the first person to hear it.

"I *adore* it," Melissa says dramatically.

I wish that girl would shut up.

But she doesn't. She steps closer to Eddie and says, "Isn't it pretty?"

I want him to say *NO!* Not about the name but to her, like, *NO! I'm not your friend! I belong to Violet! Back off!*

Instead, he nods. "Cool. I like it."

Melissa smiles at him. "Hey, who's your teacher this year?"

"Mrs. Hughes."

"You're kidding!" she shrieks. "She's mine too! We'll be in the same class!"

Well, stab me in the heart, why don't you? First, she's stealing Lottie; next she's gonna work on Eddie. I'm sick of her. I push off the stairs and make sure I'm standing closer to Eddie than she is.

"You feel like doing something?" I say. Mainly, I do this to get his attention off Melissa. And to show her that *I* am his friend, not her.

"BrainFreeze?" He leans forward on his handlebars.

"We don't have to collect those cups, do we?" Melissa says.

I can't believe this girl. "How we gonna pay for it then?"

"It's disgusting," she says, wrinkling her nose. "I'll just ask my mom for the money."

Eddie shrugs. "Either way."

"I'll go find Lottie," I say.

"You mean 'Char,'" Melissa says. "That's who she is now."

"I know that!" I know my best friend.

"Char!" I call into the house. Calling that name makes me feel like a liar; I'm not used to it. I do like Lottie's new name, but I don't like Melissa reminding me. Maybe Lottie is staying at her house and maybe they are friends, but don't act like you know her better than I do. "Char!" I holler. "Char! Char!"

Lottie comes charging down the stairs, laughing.

"What's so funny?" I ask.

She lifts her shoulders and smiles. "I heard you keep yelling, 'Char, Char,' and I was like, 'Who's Char?'" She opens her mouth wide and stares at me. We crack up laughing.

When we get outside, Melissa asks, "What's so funny?"

"Nothing," I say, putting my arm around Lottie. "You wouldn't understand."

26

There is nothing better than a BrainFreeze to cool you off, especially when you walked all the way around the woods to the county road to get it.

We sit at a picnic table under a tree. Melissa's all persnickety about where she can sit because there's a little bird poop here and there on the bench. I don't want to sit in bird poop either, but—oh, my Lord!—don't make a big deal out of it; just scootch down a little.

We're not talking much. Mostly, we're slurping our drinks.

Then Melissa says, "I have a good idea." Her eyes gleam. "Let's play truth or dare."

Lottie—I mean, Char—claps her hands. "Okay! Think of some good questions!"

"Or some good dares," I say, looking directly at Melissa. *I dare her to . . .* This has got to be good. I think on this.

"I got a good one!" Lottie yells. "Melissa, truth or dare?"

Melissa smiles. "Truth."

Lottie leans forward and asks, "If *Paris Heights* was your real life, and Zeke went to our school and got into a terrible accident and had amnesia, would you tell him you were his girlfriend and that he had always loved you?"

"Who's Zeke?" Eddie and I say together.

"Like only the best-looking guy on *Paris Heights*," Melissa says and laughs. Then she turns to Lottie. "You know I would! Do you even have to ask?"

They giggle together. A slow burn creeps up from my heart and works up to my eyes.

"Okay, okay, my turn," Melissa says. "Char— truth or dare?"

"Truth."

Melissa's not prepared. I finish my BrainFreeze, it takes her so long to come up with the lame question she asks, which is this: "If your sisters were held for ransom and your parents had been kidnapped and the only way you could save them was to fling yourself off a cliff with only your long wedding dress for a parachute, would you do it?"

Eddie groans.

Lottie considers this question seriously. "Yes, I would do it."

Melissa looks sympathetically at her.

"Oh, my Lord!" This is like boxing with pillows. "I can't believe you're asking these questions. Come on, let's play it right." I look at Lottie. "I got a good one for you. Truth or dare?"

"Truth!" She's into it now.

"Who's your best friend?"

Her face falls. Everything stops—the smiling, the laughing, the birds' singing—everything stops and Lottie stares at me as if I asked her to pluck the still-beating heart from someone she loves.

"Violet . . . ," she says, but she's not answering the question. Her eyes plead with me to stop.

"Answer the question," I say. She asked for the truth, now she's got to give it.

The air is thick. I wait.

"Okay, this is my answer," she finally says. "Violet is my oldest and dearest best friend."

Ha! I knew it!

"And Melissa is my newest best friend."

"That's not an answer!" I say. "You have to pick one!"

"You think you're so tough," Melissa says. "I've

got the perfect dare for you, if you're not too scared to take it."

"I ain't scared of anything you can dish out," I say. "Go ahead!"

"Okay." She smirks. "I dare you to kiss Eddie."

The expression on my face freezes. My heart falls inside of me, crashing a hundred times. Lottie looks shocked. Eddie looks shocked too, but in a truer way, like the way he looked when we were sitting on the porch and we felt that lightning strike the woodpecker tree.

My eyes flash back to Melissa. She has a face full of smug. I want to push that smug back into her. I stomp over to Eddie, grab his shirt, and smash my lips into his. Then I push him away and look triumphantly at Melissa.

"There!" I say. "I did it—I kissed him! It was nothing."

I say that to let her know how little her dare means to me. But when I look at their faces, I see I've done everything wrong. I quickly turn to Eddie, but he's already standing up, turning away, leaving.

"Eddie, wait!" I desperately glance from them to Eddie. He keeps walking, head down. I jog behind him. "I'm sorry. I didn't mean—"

He starts running.

There ain't no catching up to him now.

Some kind of weight presses in on me. My shoulders sag. My eyes hurt from behind. I look back to the picnic table, back to two sets of wide eyes staring at me. I glance the other way, to Eddie, who's not there anymore. Catching a ragged breath, I drop my head and slink home through the woods.

27

I have betrayed Eddie with a kiss. I am a Judas.

The whole thing plays over and over in my mind: Melissa, sneering at me, daring me to kiss Eddie; my jaw dropping open; Lottie's hand flying to cover her mouth. But the face that means the most to me is Eddie's. His eyes got big and round, but his face had a gentle look. Tears well up in my eyes when I think about his face. Oh, my Lord, I can't believe the thing I've done.

I'm hiding out in my room. Momma's making supper. She thinks I'm reading a book, but I can't concentrate on nothing 'cept what happened. I didn't mean to hurt Eddie. I just wanted to shut Melissa up. But even as I was doing that, even when I slid my eyes over to see her defeat, I remember noticing his lips. I didn't know a boy's lips could be so soft.

It don't matter now. He hates me. He'll never be my friend again, and I don't blame him.

I wrap my arms around my knees. I sit like that for a long time, until I hear the phone ring and Momma call up, "Violet, phone!"

I got no idea who'd want to call me. Maybe it's a wrong number. My heart starts up. Maybe it's Eddie's parents calling to yell at me. I don't want Momma to know about this, so I rush down the stairs to the kitchen, grab the phone, and drag it as far as the cord will let me. "Hello?"

"Violet, it's me."

I sink to the floor hearing Lottie's voice. "Hey." I'll let her yell at me too. Lord knows I deserve it.

But she doesn't yell. Her voice sounds lonely. "Why did you ask me that question?"

The thing with Eddie is taking up such a big place in my head, it takes me a minute to remember what she's talking about. "It's okay," I say. "You can like her better than me."

"I don't like her better than you! Wait a second." The rustle of the cord comes through, then her voice lowers. "You've been acting weird ever since Melissa moved here."

"No, I haven't—you have, with all your makeup and magazines, plus now you got a bra." I hear her sigh when I say that. "You keep talking about boys being cute. You even said that about Eddie."

"Eddie *is* cute—haven't you ever noticed? And I know you think I'm doing whatever Melissa tells me to do, but I'm not. I'm doing what I want to do."

My eyes narrow even though she can't see me. "What about *Paris Heights* and all that stuff?"

She clicks her tongue. "I don't care about that! It's just fun because Melissa's so into it."

"So she *is* your best friend now."

"Violet, would you stop it? Besides, why can't I have two best friends? You have me and Eddie."

My heart wells up with sadness. "Not anymore I don't."

"Oh." She lowers her voice and whispers, "What are you going to do?"

"I don't know. He don't want to be friends no more."

"You don't know that!"

I remember him running away from me. He knows I can't catch up to him when he runs full speed. "Yes, I do," I say. What I said about kissing him was past forgiving. If I were him, I would erase Violet Raines forever. When I saw the person that used to be her, I'd see right through her, like she was nothing but air. "He'll never talk to me again."

We are quiet for a few minutes. Then Lottie says, "What did it feel like?"

I push the phone closer to my face. "What?"

"When you kissed him," she says. "What did it feel like?"

"I don't know!" I holler. God Almighty, I'm grievous about this problem and that's what she asks me. I ain't going to tell her about his soft lips and his boy smell. Or the strange-good feeling it gave me when we kissed.

When I don't say nothing, she says, "Well, you can't just not be friends anymore. You've known him all your life."

For a moment, I see Eddie with his fish doll and its worn-out fins, Eddie on his bike riding that wheelie, and I think of Lottie and me carving our names into her bedpost. I feel like crying. All that I've given up, just to show Melissa. I am foolish.

"Are you still there?" Lottie asks.

"Yeah," I say, but my heart is about half a mile away, down the road off the turn.

28

Lord Almighty, someone's banging on the front door, and Momma's not even done frying our eggs yet.

"I'll get it," I say. Don't often get a knock this early, 'specially on a Saturday morning. I swing the door open and there's Lottie standing on the porch. Melissa too. I don't want Momma hearing any of what happened yesterday, so I slip out, closing the door behind me. "Hey," I say and look down.

"Look!" is all Lottie says. She pushes a folded newspaper into my hands.

Okay, I see the president is doing something. "So?" I hand it back to her. I wonder if they came to make more of a fool out of me than I did myself.

"No, no!" they yell together.

Lottie takes the paper from me and opens it so's the front page is full. "Here!" She points with one hand. They exchange a glance as I take the paper.

All the breath is knocked out of me. Me and Lottie, on the front page! "Oh, my Lord!" I stare, astonished. I can't believe we are front-page news. Only your most important news gets on the front page.

Lottie jumps up and down. "Read it, read it!" But before I can, she's already telling me what it says. "Everything we said is right here in the paper! And the Home Sweet Home people are going to fix everything! And they're raising money for us to replace stuff!"

"All right!" Melissa says and they high-five.

I'm not even annoyed; I am in shock.

I'm staring at us, me and Lottie. In the picture, we're leaning against each other, and Lottie's arm is around me. We're both smiling these huge smiles, the kind that squish your eyes and make your cheeks big, and anyone could see just by looking how good friends we are.

And just in case there was any doubt, the head-line reads "Best Friends Survive Strike." Well, there it is, God's honest truth, right there in the newspaper—*Best Friends.*

Lottie is still talking.

Melissa makes a fist and sticks it under Lottie's

mouth like it was a microphone. "Char, you've survived lightning and now you're on the front page of the newspaper. What's next for you?"

I can't help it; I accidentally let myself laugh.

Lottie says, "There's even more!"

She grabs the paper and flips it over for me. I look where the story's continued inside, and there's a little picture of Lottie, me, and Melissa, but not the one where I let my mad face show. The photographer must have taken this picture when we weren't looking. I'm standing in the middle, pointing to something far in the distance. And even though Melissa's leaning against the banister and Lottie's sitting, we're all looking ahead to the same thing. I wish I knew what it was.

"Oh, my Lord!" I say. I hug the newspaper to me. I love this article, and I love these pictures. A wonderful feeling swells up in me, and I feel like I'm going to burst.

Lottie hugs me and says, "All this is because of you! That letter you wrote!"

I look at Melissa's face in the picture and then glance at the real Melissa. "Actually, I kind of got the idea from you." She looks a little surprised when I say that, but I feel it's right to give credit where credit is due. I go on. "You know, how you write all those Hollywood letters and you put your picture in." I turn to Lottie. "That's how I got the idea."

"All right!" Lottie holds her hands up, one high five for each of us. We slap her hands and giggle.

Melissa grabs a pen from her pocket and offers it to me. "Sign it, Violet." She holds the pen out and looks me directly in the eyes. "I've just decided to start a collection of local celebrities." She clicks the pen. "You'll be my first."

She's not laughing as I take the pen and neither am I. This is a peace treaty. Everyone's quiet as I write my name carefully across the picture. I don't even realize I'm holding my breath and they are too, until I lift the pen and we all let our breath go at the same time.

When I look up, Lottie is smiling at me, and Melissa is blowing on my autograph so it don't smear. Lottie is still Lottie, even though she's Char now. And Melissa, with her makeup and all her Detroit bragging, ain't that bad. She has some good ideas and she's a fast runner, I saw that the day of the alligator.

I saw another thing that day too. One person who didn't run away. My heart is full of sorrow on how I treated him. I can't run away either. I got to find him.

29

I tell Lottie and Melissa what I got to do. After I say good-bye to Momma, Melissa and Lottie walk with me a little ways, then they head back to Melissa's house.

I'm on my own now, walking toward Eddie's house, practicing what I'll say when I knock on his door. If I say sorry, what if he doesn't forgive me? Better to not apologize—then he can't not-forgive me. Maybe I could act like I'm so happy and tell him about the newspaper and how everything's being fixed, and—

And then I see him, just hitting the curve before the woods. "Eddie!" I yell.

He turns and sees me. Then he whirls around and takes off toward the woods.

I start running too. "Eddie! Eddie!"

I'm rounding the curve, but he's way ahead of me, already slipping into the woods.

"Wait!" I shout. But I know waiting for me's not

part of his plan. He wants to get away from me. He hates me. Tears sting my eyes, but I keep running.

Leaves and branches scratch me as I shoot through the trees. A spiderweb sticks to my arm.

I shudder and slap it off. I can't see him anywhere, but I dart through the trees, sticking to the path. Oaks and cypresses blur as I rush past.

I can't see the river, but I'm running alongside it on the bank when I hear the sound of chains clinking and metal stretching.

Eddie's crossing the bridge.

"Eddie, wait!" I yell. "Eddie!" But he's already gone when I come up to the bridge. The metal net sways after him, squeaking like a rusty swing.

I run up the dirt hill and climb up to the bridge. Putting my hands on the cables, I feel the weight of the bridge swing back and forth. Looking through it to the other side is like looking through a tunnel. I pull myself up and slide one foot onto the cable. My heart hollows out. My breath becomes rapid and shallow. I'm sweating everywhere. My fingers curl around the hand cables and I hoist my other foot up. The chain-link net rattles all the way down, and I swing on the cable.

I scream.

I'm losing my balance. I don't want to fall. Even

if the net catches me, I don't want to fall. The water's rushing below. It's way far down. My mind is telling my feet, "Move, move, move! Get off this bridge," but my feet ain't going nowhere. I'm stuck. I'll rot up here and they'll find a skeleton tangled in the chains.

"Eddie!" I yell with all my might. I don't hear nothing, and that hurts even worse than being stuck up here. Tears roll down my cheeks, thinking about Eddie not yelling back. My lips press together, and I sag against the net. My heart hurts. "Eddie!" I yell, my voice catching. I lose my footing and my hands rake the chains for a better hold. "Come back!" I shout. I catch sight of the black water rushing below, and I squeeze my eyes shut.

"Eddie, please!" I open my eyes and lift my voice. "I'm afraid of alligators and I'm afraid of kissing and I'M AFRAID OF CROSSING THIS BRIDGE!" I pause. "I'm sorry!"

Yelling that makes me feel better, so I yell it again. "I'm sorry!"

Silence. Then some twigs snap, and Eddie pops out from behind some bushes. He stares at me, and I swear his blue eyes are blazing a path right to me. I ain't ever noticed the full power of his eyes before.

We stare at each other like that for a minute before I remember I'm stuck on this high wire. "I can't get down," I yell. "Help me."

Eddie opens his mouth likes he's gonna say something, and I know I deserve whatever's coming, but instead he jogs to the end of the bridge and climbs up. He rattles across it surefooted, like he's got both feet on the ground.

I stare at his shoes. "Don't shake it," I say quietly. It becomes a chant: "Don't shake it.... Don't shake it.... Don't shake it," until he gets right up to me. Then he's prying my grip off.

"What are you doing?" I screech.

"You got to let go," he says.

"NO!" I don't want to fall. I don't want to cross this bridge.

"You'll be all right," he says, loosening my fingers from the chain. "But you got to let go."

When he gets my fingers loose, his hand is holding mine. His hand holds mine real tight. Then he turns me around so's I'm facing the way I came, and he puts my hand back on the net. I can't hardly walk; I'm still scared, but I inch my feet forward until I come up to the end, and I leap off with Eddie leaping behind me.

I don't know what he's going to say to me. I think about what I said, what I said after I kissed him, and I hang my head.

"Well?" he says, and I look up at him. His eyes burn with their full power.

God Almighty, it's like I never seen his eyes before.

"What?" he says. "What?" He kind of grins and the power turns into a twinkle.

I didn't know eyes could do that.

For a moment, I don't know what to say. Finally, I look straight at him and ask, "What do we do now?"

He reaches toward my face and my heart pounds like it did on the bridge, but all I feel is a light touch as he brushes a leaf out of my hair. Time stretches out before he says anything.

"I'm hot," he says.

I wipe the back of my neck. "Yeah, me too."

"BrainFreeze?"

All my nerves fire up. "I can't cross that bridge."

"I know," he says. He looks at me real steady. "We'll take the long way around."

That suits me just fine.

30

Open House at the junior high is like a party. Everyone you know is there, and the teachers got snacks and drinks out and everyone's all smiling. They ain't got me fooled; I know this is still school. They're just trying to warm us up. I eat all the cookies I can, 'cause they ain't gonna be this generous when school starts.

Momma and I rode up with Mrs. Townsend and Lottie. Lottie's got her diamond watch on and she's wearing lip gloss and she looks real pretty. When we came in, they gave us stickers to wear that say, *Hi! My name is* blank. Except of course it don't say "blank"; that's where you write your name in. Lottie's sticker says, *Hi! My name is Char.* She has written it in real good cursive.

Each teacher has a table with handouts and such. Mrs. Townsend and Lottie go in search of her teacher. My teacher's got an easy name, Mrs. Nash, and Momma and I spot her right away. When Mrs. Nash realizes we're walking up to her table, she squints in on my name tag and then her face looks all surprised.

"Violet Raines," she says, coming from around the table. She sticks her hand out to me and I shake it. Her hand's bigger than mine, but the shake is just right—not too firm, and plus she doesn't hold on to my hand when the shake is over like some ladies at church do.

She shakes Momma's hand too, but then turns right back to me. "Violet, I'm Mrs. Nash, and I've been waiting all day to meet you."

She's serious. My eyebrows scrunch up, and I look straight at her. "Why?"

"You're going to be my first guest speaker! We'll be studying lightning and electricity in science. I saw you in the newspaper, found your name on my class list, and I thought, 'This is serendipity.'"

"Serendipity?" It sounds like ice cream being scooped on a summer day.

She nods. "'Serendipity' means a stroke of good luck. It's a great word."

I think so too. I tuck this word into my brain so's I can write it down later and save it in my shoe box. Looking at her, I decide right then and there she's all right. Well, you can't help but like another word collector, even if she is a teacher.

She goes back around her table, and Momma and I walk up to it. A big envelope has my name on it, and Mrs. Nash starts pulling things out of it. "Here's a map of the school and the portables; you'll want to walk around today and see where everything is. Let's see, locker combination, gym combination, oh, and here's your lunch pass." She hands me a bright blue plastic card with my name on it. "You'll have to show this every time you walk into the cafeteria for lunch."

Then she says to Momma, "We have six lunch shifts this year, a different color for each shift; it's the only way we can make sure that the children are where they're supposed to be."

Momma nods. They start talking about over-crowding and boring stuff like that.

"Violet!" It's Lottie! I turn around, but there's so many kids running around, I don't see her. My eyes become lasers, scanning the crowd. No Lottie. Turning back, I listen to Momma and Mrs. Nash. They're talking about my schedule now.

"Violet!" Eddie! I whip my head around in the direction of his voice.

At first, I don't see him; I don't see anyone

except strangers. Then Lottie and Eddie and Melissa come through the crowd, holding up bright blue cards like trophies. Oh Lord, my heart swells up like a hot air balloon. I shoot my hand up, waving my own blue card. My friends make their way toward me. I start for them, but Momma pulls me back. "Honey, Mrs. Nash just asked you a question."

"Sorry, ma'am," I say to my teacher, using my good-manners voice.

"That's all right," she says and smiles. "It's very busy in here." She leans forward and pats my hand. "So, how do you feel about starting junior high?"

I glance at my friends, their smiling faces and their blue cards, and I look back to Mrs. Nash. "I am jubilant," I say.

And that is no taradiddle.

Acknowledgments

Here we are at the end of the book, and I'd like to thank the people who helped me along the way: God Almighty, for one; Ted Malawer, my wonderful agent; Brooke Haworth, who shared her lightning experience with me; Sandra Friend, Joan Jarvis, and Steve Rajtar for sharing their swinging bridge experiences with me; Michelle Carr, who read and commented on the earlier drafts; and Steve Haworth, who read the early drafts, the later drafts, and who stayed up way too late with me talking about lightning and alligators.

Finally, I want to thank Stacy Cantor, my editor at Walker Books for Young Readers. Stacy was one of the first people to meet Violet, and she recognized her immediately. Her keen insight and vision for the story were an inspiration to me. I couldn't have found a better friend or a better home for Violet.